Prue Carmichael was born in Brighton. She has lived in Spain, Paris and Nepal, and she has led an extensive and varied career in film-making. She writes full time, currently hopping between Notting Hill Gate and Morocco.

GW00649245

The Windfall

PRUE CARMICHAEL

A *Warner* Book

First published in Great Britain
by Warner Books in 1996

Copyright © Prue Carmichael 1996

The moral right of the author has been asserted.

*All characters in this publication are fictitious
and any resemblance to real persons, living or dead,
is purely coincidental.*

All rights reserved.
No part of this publication may be reproduced,
stored in a retrieval system, or transmitted, in any
form or by any means, without the prior
permission in writing of the publisher, nor be
otherwise circulated in any form of binding or
cover other than that in which it is published and
without a similar condition including this
condition being imposed on the subsequent purchaser.

A CIP catalogue record for this book
is available from the British Library.

ISBN 0 7515 1641 4

Typeset by Hewer Text Composition Services, Edinburgh
Printed and bound in Great Britain by
Clays Ltd, St. Ives plc

Warner Books
A Division of
Little, Brown and Company (UK)
Brettenham House
Lancaster Place
London WC2E 7EN

To Jo, Frannie and Matthew, and
of course Phillipa Scott and Kate
Mitson, with thanks.

CHAPTER ONE

IT WAS MIDSUMMER, the drowsy lull of afternoon, when no sensible Spaniard moved. Above the deserted coast road, a great rock jutted from the mountainside like the skull of a guillotined giant. The locals called the rock El Bueno, the Good One, but despite its benign name they crossed themselves when they looked up, marvelling at how it retained its precarious hold through wind and heat and winter storms. No birds flew and it seemed the giant too was dozing in the hot sun, unmoved by the bustle of a fast-moving beach buggy as it rounded a bend on the road far below. It slowed down and came to a stop at a lay-by on the edge of the cliff. A slight, dark woman wearing a T-shirt and white trousers got out. She stretched, and lifted her hair from the nape of her neck. For a moment she shaded her eyes with her hand and looked up at the forbidding, granite features, staring at the hot sky. The smell of wild thyme crushed by the buggy's wheels rose around her. She let her hand drop and lit a cigarette. The click of her lighter and slight tick of the engine were the only sounds in the simmering heat. She gave a deep breath, grateful for the silence. For Minou, hell would probably be somewhere where the noise went on and on. If, at the end of life, they sent her through the wrong door, she was sure it would be to spend eternity in a disco. Not that all silences were peaceful. Some could be as brutal as noise. Lonely, city silences, sad Sunday mornings and the indifferent soundlessness of a phone that would never ring again with a call from the voice she loved. But the silence on the *bojeo* road had no particular tone except a demand for total submission to the time of day.

'A bit of peace and quiet, a break in the sun.' The unexpected invitation from her half-sister Bitty was brusque, almost a command, issued in a loud, unmusical voice that hadn't softened in twenty years.

'Yes, you could probably do with a rest.' Bitty's afterthought sounded like an accusation rather than concern. Minou, too astonished to think, accepted the ungracious invitation obediently. As one always did with Bitty. There followed no expression of pleasure at the thought of their reunion, just the briefest of instructions as to how and where Minou could find the house.

'You'd better get a taxi or hire a car at the airport or something.' Bitty's final orders before hanging up.

The beach buggy was the only vehicle available in Malaga, or so they said. The hire charge was exorbitant but Minou took it. Life, she believed, was to be lived flat out until some great hand in the sky yanked it away, so there was no point in quibbling about necessary extravagances. Well aware that her over-optimistic nature often led to disappointment, she started off along the Costa del Sol road in high spirits. No sensible person should dwell on what could go wrong, in case by brooding one would make it happen. The important thing was now, the moment, and whatever came next. And this was a holiday, an invitation from Bitty after twenty years of silence. It must mean something. After all, Bitty was older now: forty-eight, or was it forty-nine? Minou could never remember if it was six or seven years that separated them. And with age people mellowed, became more tolerant. And Bitty was family, after all, even if they were joined only by the slenderest of threads in sharing their notorious father whom one reviled and the other revered. Family. Like so many people who have none, it was to Minou an almost sacred word which made her feel as if someone had thrown a silk shawl around her slim shoulders. With no more than a small holdall, a beach basket on the driver's seat and a duty-free bottle of Mitsouko for Bitty, she made good time along the coast road rather than the motorway. But after a few kilometres of merciless urbanisation, the ugliness of self-catering developments and monstrous skyscraper apartments dumped along the sea's edge like great slices of white cheese, her joy began to dwindle. As she passed the oil-refineries outside Algeciras, belching into the hot sky, childhood memories, like little bits of dust ignored in corners, began to blow across her thoughts. It was the voice. That one brief phone call told her Bitty hadn't changed. That voice which had always begun each declaration with, 'Well, I always blame . . .' That voice that had assured her years ago that she'd 'be found dead in a ditch someday'. This dire prophecy was hurled at her when it was discovered that at the age of sixteen she'd lost her virginity in a bus shelter on Hastings promenade – without a quiver of regret. Even now, Minou giggled, more interested in recalling the event than anything Bitty had had to say about it. Which was a lot. Her partner in crime had been a trapeze artist from the visiting summer circus. One of a troupe of four brothers, 'The Golden Apollos'. Oh, how blond and beautiful and brave they were! Danish, Swedish? No, they were Finnish, that was it, Finnish. Of course, what Bitty never ever found out was that Minou had slept (if that was the right word for steamy encounters on the shingle at low-tide and passionate embraces in the backs of bumper cars) with all of them, and found each one delightful. Different but delightful. From that heady summer Minou knew sex was one of the most enjoyable encounters one could ever have.

But not so Bitty, who'd never been too keen on sex and poured scorn on anything pertaining to romance, even though she was, by that time, an air hostess. She flew round the world in her smart uniform, only coming home to Hastings to regale her mother, Helen, and Minou, her young half-sister with the glories of five-star hotels in every capital city, as well as recounting outraged case histories of her bottom being pinched by businessmen in first-class. 'Well, I always blame . . .'

'Why is she so angry all the time . . .?' Minou asked Helen as she wandered up and down her narrow little Hastings garden snipping heads off sweetpeas.

'She's probably disappointed, dear. She wanted to be an actress, you know, but I think Cody put her off. She never said so, but I think that's what happened. Take no notice.' Helen, whose eyes were as calm and grey as the south of England sea on a quiet day, had long since found it best to take no notice of anything unpleasant. Especially anything to do with her ex-husband, Cody, who inevitably brought trouble and disruption for her and for his disparate daughters.

* * *

Whether out of disappointment, rage or just grabbing at the lifestyle she thought to be her due, Bitty became Mrs Nolan, wife of one of the rich, first-class businessmen she had tended in flight. She and Minou had already drifted far apart and the news was relayed to Minou, now living in Paris, on a series of Christmas cards from Helen.

'Bitty's got married. In Hong Kong, I think.'

'Bitty's living in Marbella. She seems more settled in Spain.'

'Bitty's had a little boy. But she's getting divorced.' The brief bulletins arrived in neat handwriting beneath robins, reindeer and a line from 'Hark the Herald Angels Sing'. The last card Minou could remember said that Bitty had left Marbella and was living further up the coast in Cody's old house. Then, twenty years of silence.

Minou finished her cigarette, carefully extinguishing every spark in case the sapless grass ignited. She reached into the car for her sunglasses and glanced at her modest luggage. She had always travelled light, it was almost a point of pride to do so, but Bitty would be sure to remark on it as if she were a refugee.

'*C'est tout?*' Helen, so kind and doing her best had grasped at a bit of schoolgirl French when Minou, aged seven, was delivered to her terrace house in Hastings by Cody's PA. '*C'est tout*' was a tattered toy parrot and the cotton frock she stood up in. The child nodded and offered Helen the last crumbs of a bar of chocolate.

'*Oui, Madame*,' replied Minou, who had no idea who this lady was.

'Oh, dear . . .' said Helen faintly, and re-read the letter

the PA had handed over with the child from the back of a rented Rolls Royce. It was from Cody, her ex-husband, met and married within a few days when she had been in the WRENS and he an assistant director on the film *In Which We Serve*.

'Oh, Cody, Cody, how could you *do* this to me?' Although their separation and subsequent divorce had been almost as rapid as their marriage, Helen was still astonished, but no longer hurt, by her ex-husband's excesses. The child recognised the word 'Cody' and caught sight of a photo of him tucked away behind a lot of others on an upright piano. It was the same picture Maman had had beside her bed, back home in Martinique. The picture that she gazed at as she was dying.

'Cody!' the child exclaimed. 'Papa!'

Helen gloomily accepted this as proof. 'Yes, dear. Now, what about some tea?'

'Who's *she*?' Bitty, thirteen years old, pink, white and plump and smelling danger, exploded back from Hastings High School, flung her satchel on the cretonne sofa and glared at the small intruder.

'Hush,' said Helen, who now knew exactly who Minou was from Cody's imploring twelve-page letter. With no address. In which he told her that she, of all the women he had ever loved, was the only one with a vestige of humanity in her heart – for all that she'd been to Roedean. The child's mother (here followed the sketchiest of explanations as to how they'd met while he was shooting *The Private Life of Napoleon* on Martinique, hence the child's real name – Josephine) had tragically died. And he was leaving for Alaska. He promised Helen that his PA would keep in touch. And PS, the child's nickname was Minou and she was a nice little thing.

'Well?' demanded Bitty, bristling to the ends of her yellow pigtails.

'She's, er, your sister . . . in way,' explained Helen who thought she might as well get it over quickly. 'More or less.'

'What's her name? What's your name?' Bitty was outraged. Minou didn't answer. 'What's the matter with her, Mummy, doesn't she speak English?'

'No, dear, she's French . . . sort of.' Bitty stuck out her tongue. Minou shrugged her thin little shoulders and laughed. Helen groaned. War had been declared and they hadn't even had tea.

'If she's my sister, is *her* surname Cody, too?' The question was asked some way into a thick silence.

'No, dear.'

'Why not?' Bitty, although she'd seldom seen her famous father, knew the advantages of the name. Lots of the girls at school had heard of him and all the teachers, too. 'Are you sure?'

'Yes.'

'I don't like her,' Bitty growled through her second scone.

'Oh, don't be so beastly. What's she done to you? She's an orphan, more or less, so just try to be nice. You might as well since she's staying.' Helen's heart went out to the watchful waif struggling with kipper fillets. 'Just for a while, anyway,' she added but with little conviction.

'But Mummy, she's *black*!'

'Bitty, that's quite enough of that! How could you even say such a thing? And anyway, it's not true.'

'Well, she's not white,' said Bitty.

A car passed on the road and then an old bus. The

afternoon was giving way. Lulled by the unviolated calm of the *bojeo,* Minou lit another cigarette. South of the road, the valley of cork trees slipped on down to where the Straits split Africa from Europe and two seas, two cultures and two continents converged. Jebel Moussa rose like a massive iguana on the Moroccan side, every crack and crumple in its sheer face sharp in the clear light. She could see the houses on the far coast scattered like fragments of torn paper, and far beyond, where the blue hill ridges stretched in waves as far back as the Middle Atlas. She'd heard that when the levante blew up from the Sahara, Jebel Moussa dissolved into a grey blur, could vanish for days, hidden by the wind, and Africa became no more than a myth. Looking over at the dark continent she supposed she should have had big thoughts about Africa but as usual found none to summon. A ferry steamed quietly towards Tangier, where later the lights would glint across the water. She felt something gentle as a prayer steal through her and, now calm, put out her second cigarette with the same careful ritual. She checked Bitty's instructions again. Only about another two kilometres and then she would see Cody's house. Somewhere he had actually lived. She took two deep breaths then got into the car. As she turned the key in the ignition she looked up again at El Bueno, as if asking permission to continue.

A grotto of pale plants grew quietly, hidden in the shade of El Bueno. To an untrained eye they might have looked no more than a clump of weeds, but set out in a more orderly way than nature would have chosen. Not a tag or label indicated what anything was, yet Titus Nolan knew every stem, leaf and petal as intimately as a man knows the woman he loves. All were thriving happily. The only one that had given him any trouble was the mandrake. Stolen from Kew; one quick thrust of a trowel, a flip into a plastic bag, then tucked into his sock. Easy as that and it hadn't murmured, let alone shrieked. Of course, it did grow locally but this way was more fun. Once on Spanish soil, however, it got its own back with a little sulky shrivelling. He sprinkled it with dried blood, bone-meal and Panadol. Although he drew the line at singing to it himself, he indulged it with Kate Bush (which for some unfathomable reason it seemed to like), and read it extracts from *The Long Dark Teatime of the Soul*. That did the trick and now, between its shield-shaped leaves, he could just make out a mysterious, peach-sized, orange seed. Wild rosemary shivered, its flowers white against the shadows; deadly nightshade flourished without fuss and the castor-oil plant promised to become quite a decent-sized shrub. Titus stroked the mandrake leaves, tested the soil with the palm of his hand, moist from a nearby spring. Well satisfied, he emerged into the bright light. With a dozen long-legged strides he reached the bulbous lips of the giant, climbed on and sprawled across the granite head. He stared at the sun. He was also listening to flamenco on his Walkman. Someone said, or he'd read somewhere, that staring at the sun was good for the sinuses. But for him it was a game: Titus against the sun. A game he invariably lost. The white circle blazed through his pupils to his brain. The clack of castanets collided behind his watering eyes and he couldn't tell if the buleria was twanging in his head or surging up from the rock into his body. He gritted his teeth until, defeated, his lids dropped. But for a moment the sun was still there, a black disc centred in a web of quivering pink veins. The sun had won again. Parched and dry

Titus reached for a bottle of warm Perrier he'd meant to give to the plants, soaked his dark, curly hair, his neck, his face and shirt. The water felt cool and good. It dried fast, tightening the long-healed scar on the side of his face. The side everyone said there was nothing wrong with. He splashed himself with the last drops in the bottle, then rose. Long legs together, chest thrown out, back slightly arched and raising his arms into a graceful curve, the tall young man began to dance on top of El Bueno.

It wasn't a classic buleria, because he'd never been taught. It wasn't very British for a man to dance and his mother, Bitty, would certainly have none of it. But ever since he was a child he'd watched. At the Feria, in the cafés and on TV, the familiar, raucous clamour told him to circle his wrists, fingers spread, take a deliberate step, scuff the rock with the ball of his foot, tap the heel of his boot. Leisurely and severe at first, he advanced upon some unseen adversary until the rhythm broke into an unpredictable clatter. Impelled, he cupped his hands, clapped, turned, stamped and strutted round the smooth brow of the giant. The harsh cries of the gypsies applauded as he drubbed and banged closer and closer to the rock's edge until, with an abrupt shout, the tape clicked off. A gecko froze and fled. A pebble dropped two hundred feet. Titus threw himself down, desperately wishing he'd brought a beer. There was plenty at the house below. It was his home, but he never played flamenco there. It looked tranquil enough but he knew that was only a temporary state. Bitty could return at any moment, in any sort of mood. She was late, which was odd. She was usually home by lunchtime, bellowing for a gin and tonic. Not that her lateness bothered him, but no one, not even she, stayed any longer than they had to in Gibraltar. He shifted into a sitting position and looked towards the Rock, as it was called, its hideous hump mercifully hidden by the slopes of the *bojeo*. He hated Gibraltar. It was to him a multilingual, bi-national mistake, like himself. He never went near the place except to sprint on and off the London plane. Even then he tried to hold his breath from the border to the airport and, if addressed, responded only in sign language. To give her her due, Bitty didn't like it either and only went to restock every month at Safeway's. But she'd been three times in under two weeks, which was odd. The only reason Titus could think of was that she'd found a new bar where they gave unlimited credit. Even so, he decided to forget about the beer; for a little longer the house could drowse in peace among the cork trees.

La Preciosa was said to have been built in the eighteenth century by a pirate. Set among smaller buildings, all with terracotta roof tiles weathered to a soft grey, E-shaped, its arms stretched either side of a courtyard. It was less sheltered than the usual Spanish house but a perfect lookout over the Straits.

'It's absolutely true . . . a real pirate!' Bitty, tinkling glass in hand and tossing her blonde hair, never tired of boasting to those who hadn't heard and some who had. It was like a tape that Titus could mouth along with.

'That's why Cody bought it. He was making *The Battle of Trafalgar* for Paramount, or was it MGM? Anyway, he got it for a song . . . but then, of course, Cody was quite a pirate too.' She always referred to her late father as Cody, an irritating affectation she'd picked up from the Press who'd shrieked his exploits second only to those of Errol Flynn. 'New Romance for Cody! This Time It's For Ever.' Which usually meant about six months. His mother's proprietary smirk sickened him. She loathed his grandfather with all her heart. She'd only ever seen two of his films (which she hated) and furthermore she'd denounce in a flash anyone she suspected of being a buccaneer. And she hated the house. It was for this that Titus could find no forgiveness.

'Oh yes, where was I? The pirate . . .' Refuelled, Bitty was unstoppable. 'Well, every time he saw a galleon founder, he'd light a beacon on the hill, his men would row out, plunder away and he got madly rich and bought up most of Andalusia. That's what they say. And they also say there's buried treasure in the garden. Titus used to look everywhere when he was little. Didn't you, darling?' She used to call him 'darling' from time to time when there were visitors. 'So sweet, with his little bucket and spade.'

The dogs, dotted in slumbering groups around the courtyard, were the first to hear the beach buggy. As one they rose, an ill-assorted pack: a greyhound, two Jack Russells, two mongrel bitches – as fat as bus conductresses – and an ancient Peke. Meaningless barks tore the air as they stationed themselves under the big fig tree outside the front door. Titus, alerted, screwed his fists into a telescope. It must be Minou, his half-aunt, step-aunt or whatever, arriving. Bitty couldn't stand her. Bitty's dislike of this seldom mentioned relative was so intense, Titus could only assume she'd been invited because she might be good for a few grand. Bitty hadn't even considered going to meet her, or given a thought about being there to greet her. Already, Titus felt Minou to be an ally. He considered going down and doing the polite thing with his impeccable, public school manners which were always on hand when needed. He decided against it. Alert as a young bird of prey, he watched and waited. Antonio, the gardener, his straw hat like a blob of pale butter, waved the hose at the hanging baskets of Lobelia which Bitty, in her poor Spanish which cleaved one's head in two, insisted were watered twice a day. Antonio grumbled back in his Andalusian slur.

'*What* I ask you?' she yelled. 'What do you think I pay you for?' Aggrieved as a Goya martyr, Antonio reminded her that she hadn't paid him for three months. Juanita, Antonio's black-clad wife, who'd been there since Cody's day, usually joined them, slipping in a hapless plea for a new washing-machine.

'I'm not made of money. Oh, you take advantage, you really do. No one else would put up with it,' Bitty would complain. But they put up with it. Had done so for twenty years. Bitty felt all the better for a good shout. Antonio grudgingly watered the plants and Juanita continued to pray for a new washing-machine.

The dogs raised the levels of their barks as the beach buggy came into sight. A beach buggy, that was a plus. With growing interest, Titus watched as the front wheels squashed Antonio's hose and came to a halt at an angle which would block Bitty's sweep into the garage with her Range Rover. Bitty wouldn't like that. Another plus. Minou got out. The dogs leaped and jumped. She neither flinched from them, nor made any attempt to ingratiate herself with nervous pats as most people did. Titus was glad of that. Not that she was in any danger from that ponderous lot. But he had been careless once, paid the price and paid it fast. A growl, a snarl, a wet, pink mouth, white teeth and he was blinded by blood in his eyes and screaming out for help. He watched her light a cigarette. Another plus.

Minou looked round for a moment, then approached

the house with a swift, tentative step, one shoulder raised as if she was about to break into a little tap dance. Even at this distance it seemed to him she had a talent for controlling the space around herself without being aloof. Juanita appeared from the front door. Minou shook hands with her and Juanita immediately embraced her on both cheeks. Deprived of water, Antonio ambled over and carried Minou's luggage into the house.

Titus slipped a cassette into the Walkman. Despite his thirst and overwhelming curiosity he decided not to go down just yet.

CHAPTER TWO

HER ROOM WAS at the far end of the eastern arm of the house. The part that had, in the old days, been used to house overflow guests. It hadn't been decorated since Cody's day but despite the flaking paint it felt solid, with three-foot walls and a thick wooden floor. The door, with black hinges and a round handle, opened on to the small room with a large carved wardrobe, a table with a mirror, a child's painted chair and a blue rug. Above the old-fashioned bed was a metal ring from which had once hung a mosquito net. It was serene as a nun's cell except for the bedside light, a silly china dolphin with its mouth open, and a shelf of tatty paperbacks left by other second-best guests. Juanita opened the doors of a French window leading on to a small balcony. Minou gazed at Jebel Moussa's bulk framed between faded pale blue curtains.

'*Aqui . . . aqui . . .*' Juanita bustled her into the bathroom. It was high-ceilinged with an enormous, old-fashioned tub and the most complicated layout of the thickest pipes Minou had ever seen. Juanita tried to explain the whims of the plumbing. Apparently, from what Minou could gather with her limited Spanish, the water depended on the weather. If the wind came from the south, it gushed, although it did have a tendency to stop mid-flow. If it came from the east, the best one could expect was a trickle. Juanita turned on the big, brass tap. There were anguished noises far away but nothing happened. She banged a pipe and was rewarded by a rush of rusty water. Whichever way the wind blew, the best thing was to bang something. Juanita assured her she'd soon get the hang of it. Drawn by the mystery of the Moroccan coastline, Minou went back into the bedroom and stepped on to the balcony.

'Look!' said Juanita and pointed to a swallow's nest tucked into the eaves. 'You come the same time as the swallows.' This seemed to please her. Minou shortened her gaze and looked down on to the garden. Two rows of cypress trees led from either side of crumbling steps down to what had once been a smooth lawn. It was now yellow and pockmarked with bumps where the dogs had buried bones. There was a fountain in the middle, long dead and encrusted with dried slime and bird droppings. Beside it stood a statue of a naked boy with a skinny dog. Juanita sighed and told her that when Cody was there the lawn was green as spinach and the fountain sparkled with joy.

'*Hoy . . . mucho economía . . .*' She shook her head, looking sadly at Antonio's attempts at lettuces and cabbages which spindled their way into the boundary. She patted Minou's hand and told her that Señora Bitty would be back. '*Más tarde . . . más tarde,*' and Titus would be back '*más tarde,* as well'. She told her to rest tranquilly, patted her hand again and left her, still looking at the view as if it was a long lost lover that she pined for.

It didn't take long to unpack: one pair of white jeans, one pair of black; two T-shirts, one striped, one with roses; a pair of espadrilles; neat bedside high-heeled sandals and a cashmere shawl. That took care of her feet and the days. For the beach, messing around and the bedroom, she had her sarong wrap and then there was the dress. It was a bargain in the sale at Balmain where she still worked part-time. It wasn't one of the dresses she'd laboured over, beading, spangling and bejewelling. These were for women with rich men. This dress was a soft, coral colour crêpe de Chine, demure in the hand, but its cut an art form of seduction. She touched the lightness of the silk for reassurance then closed the warped oak door of the cupboard and sat on the edge of the bed. Almost at once, as if pushed from the inside, the door swung open again. She should wedge it but with what? Despite the brightness of the room, the glimpse of bougainvillaea from the window and the pretty light, Minou felt bereft of energy. Maybe it was the massiveness of the oak cavern which made her modest wardrobe look so sparse and uninspired. Just those few things, polite but uneasy, like guests too early for a party.

'Is that really all you've got, Minou?' she asked herself. 'Breathe in . . . breathe out.' That's what Madame always used to advise for difficult moments. Focus on the split second between the two breaths. 'Dear Madame, I'm having a wonderful time with my sister and my nephew . . .' She had an impulse to write a card, reach back to what was safe and sure. But not yet. She had no cards and, anyway, it wasn't true. If it sounded hollow, Madame would guess in a flash, and worry. Madame worried a lot about what was to become of her girls now that the Rue St Supplice was no more.

For someone who had run a Maison, Madame'd had quite a lot of surprisingly Zen-like tricks up her woolly sleeves.

'Mesdemoiselles . . .' She'd always addressed her girls as if it was a finishing school she ran above the bookshop in the Rue St Supplice. 'Peace, tranquillity . . . the essence of a true woman.' Madame would have no truck with ludicrous ideas about equality. 'That is what our gentlemen come here for and, indeed, pay for. They may not believe it to be so, but it is true, believe me. There are places elsewhere for other things.' This last was delivered with withering contempt. Breathe in . . . breathe out. Minou had learned this on her very first day at the Rue St Supplice when in all innocence she had applied for the job advertised in the bookshop down below.

'Wanted: young lady of intelligence, attractive appearance, knowledge of at least one foreign language, good education essential.' She was slightly startled to discover a hidden meaning in the ad but, philosophical and very hungry, she accepted gladly when offered by Madame, rather grandly, an opportunity to enlarge her horizon. Which was why she'd run away from Hastings in the first place. And furthermore, so far, she had enjoyed making love. But it seemed she'd got it all wrong. Love didn't come into it. Madame had started her off gently with a charming young man her own age. The son of a diplomat whose father (equally charming) had entrusted his son's initiation to her. Minou fell in love. Madame was appalled. Falling in love was ridiculous and quite out of the question. She'd had girls before who were temperamentally unsuitable but never a romantic. With a sinking heart she gave the girl a good talking to.

'But Madame, he was adorable.'

'Clients are not adorable,' snapped Madame. The girl was really too naïve to let loose – not nearly as worldly as those green eyes and slender olive limbs implied. Once again she explained the fundamental principles of the Maison and, unique as they were, those rules must be obeyed.

'Our gentlemen expect a pleasant evening, a charming companion and intelligent conversation which means mostly listening.' It was an establishment she strived to run along the lines of a literary salon, a haven from the outside world of loneliness or discontented wives. Sex was only an option. And should any of the gentlemen make even a joking reference to vestal virgins they got short shrift. Madame considered her girls special, each deserving of the good things of life but denied by circumstances. They were all well-educated and if not, she soon licked them into shape with daily doses of Molière, Victor Hugo and Racine. Thus, if any of the authorities became curious she could assure them that hers was an educational establishment.

'But no passion,' she emphasised. 'Passion leads to complications. Surely literature has taught you that?' She was about to launch into the story of *Anna Karenina* as a typical example but stopped short at the sight of Minou's tears.

'Are you going to send me away, Madame?' Minou had just escaped from the grey seas and flat light of the South of England. It would be too awful to go back. 'Please, Madame?' Madame hesitated. The girl was alone in Paris with virtually no family. Even if she had twenty brothers and sisters, she had that dangerous quality hovering between vulnerability and fanatic independence. Anything could happen to a girl like that in Paris.

'Please, Madame?' Madame had a brainwave.

'Do you know '*amlet*?'

'Sort of,' said Minou who'd done it at Hastings High.

'Read to me . . . in English.' A triumphant solution. She suggested that, in return for a little room among the rooftops, Minou read her Shakespeare every afternoon, and in the mornings help out in the rambling maisonette with light chores: replacing Champagne glasses, arranging flowers, mending lace on torn pillowcases and keeping the peace between the girls before, after and during the occasional cat-fight. This would give Madame more time to pursue her passion for literature. It was a very satisfactory arrangement all round except that it didn't pay very well. Madame took care of this, too. She had a word in the ear of one of the gentlemen who was the main accountant for Balmain. He offered Minou a job as an apprentice. It was, at first, only part-time, embroidering garments for the collection. Madame approved and said that Minou was now free to fall in love as often as she pleased as long as it was not with the house gentlemen and not on the premises. This, Minou did frequently. At least she called it love until she met Jean Luc.

He arrived with two friends, weary from a battlefront assignment. He was, one of the girls whispered to her, a war photographer. Madame's back was 'playing-up', her hair needed hennaing but, even more important, she had only two chapters left of *Wuthering Heights*. Minou received for her, a role she'd slipped into quite naturally in the last few years. How nice to see you again, Monsieur . . . Champagne? Cognac? Tea? A little whisky? Jean Luc was slow to make a request. The weary lines around his eyes told her that he'd just as soon fall asleep in front of the fire. After his friends had cheerfully departed upstairs, he stayed sitting quietly on the Louis Quinze sofa.

'More Champagne?' Minou asked him. It never did

to rush them. Give them time to talk but never ask questions about their life in the outside world. Jean Luc didn't seem the talkative type.

'*Toi*,' he said eventually. 'I would like you.' Minou shook her head. It wasn't the first time this request had been made. Madame usually dealt with it.

'I regret Monsieur, I . . . I am only the . . .' she searched for the most appropriate word. 'Administration?' she came up with. To her surprise, Jean Luc, instead of being disappointed at her refusal, trying to bend the rules or press her as some did, looked relieved. He gazed at her for a moment, detached, yet with a deep concentration as if he were about to take a photograph that might unravel a truth as yet unrevealed.

'Have dinner with me?'

'Again, Monsieur, I regret, it is against . . . 'Again she reached for a word.

'It is against the protocol.' Jean Luc threw back his head and roared with laughter. Later, he told her it was the first time he had laughed in over twenty months.

The next day she bumped into him in the flower market in St Germain and he'd offered to carry the peonies and delphiniums for her. Mindful of the rules, she refused politely but allowed him a tiny glimpse of her true regret. During the following weeks it was amazing how many times she bumped into him. Outside the staff door of Balmain one night, when she'd worked late on the Spring Collection, then in the Métro when he'd leaped on at the last moment and caught his sleeve in the door. It was this last 'coincidence' that made her realise with delight that he really was following her. She had a word with Madame who, at last, relented and gave her permission. Then, as luck would have it, he disappeared. Day after day she'd catch sight of the back of a head, the movement of an arm, only to be disappointed by a stranger's face. Until May. He was sitting in the café across the road from the back entrance when she took her lunch break. He was unshaven, leaning back in his chair, sun on his face and his eyes closed. He looked as if he'd just crawled out of hell. She crossed the road and sat down at his table.

'May I have a coffee?' she asked.

Without opening his eyes he replied, 'Champagne.'

And that night they became lovers.

The thin stream widdling into the bath tub would take about half an hour to fill, Minou reckoned. If only she'd thought to buy some cards she could fill the time by writing. 'I can see Africa from my bedroom window . . .' That, at least, was true, or she thought it was. She went on to the balcony to check the number of swallows. The chicks were squashed into the muddy little nest, their overhanging tails drooping down. The mother swallow warned her off with a long drawn out clacking cry. Minou turned, then noticed something stir on the terrace below. A black blur detached itself from the shadows. It moved across the flagstones then split into three grotesque, waddling shapes. The shapes became birds with sleek, black heads, their wing-tips serrated like the teeth of a saw. They took a flapping run, rose, wheeled and with legs hanging down, circled over the woods. They were vultures! Minou gave a sharp gasp, ran into the bathroom and slammed the door. The vultures wheeled over the approaching Range Rover as it swept round the first bend of the drive, then one by one they plopped on to its roof and rode, with Bitty, the rest of the way home.

Bitty's voice invaded every cranny of the building.

Orders, commands, endearments for the dogs, counter-orders to Antonio, followed by more loving greetings to the animals who may have been old, but weren't deaf.

'Hola! Hola! Yes, my darlings, Mummy's home. Down, boy! No, Antonio, not *there*, the kitchen, yes, yes. There's a clever girl . . . Hola!' It was like listening to an invasion. Minou held the bathroom curtain to her naked body and looked out through the steam. Bitty stood among the bags and boxes in the drive looking like a sunburst in her yellow dress. Antonio shuffled through the over-excited animals with loads of silvery plastic bags, liver, lights and other innards for the deep freeze in the dog room. He kneed and kicked his way through the outstretched, scraggy necks of the vultures pecking at the plastic bags.

'Guess what Mummy's got for din-dins, then?' Minou stepped back and shuddered. She'd been about to wave but – those awful birds. What had happened to Bitty, that rosy schoolgirl who cried through *Bambi* and used to write angry letters to mousetrap manufacturers? Minou poured oil into her bath, swirled it around and stepped in. Almost at once she was summoned.

'Minou! Minou!' Bitty's shout searched her out as she lay back in the scented water. 'Why the hell did you put that car there?' Minou curbed the impulse to obey, leap out of the bath, rush downstairs stark naked and move the wretched beach buggy.

'Josephine!' shouted Bitty. The only person who ever called her that. She slid under the water. Josephine Marguerite Latour: her names, which took her by surprise every time she had to fill in a form. Josephine because of Martinique, Marguerite because it had been Maman's name and Latour because that was Maman's name as well. She burst to the surface, unable to hold her breath any longer. There was a black crack on the white tiles that wasn't there before. Minou looked closer. A stream of ants going God knows where and back.

Bitty would be passionate about the ozone layer by now so there was no hope of any insect spray. If she asked for any she'd be ticked off for going against nature or scorned for being feeble. Oh, how Bitty could scald with scorn.

'Hastings has got an "H". Haaaaystings, you silly, or hadn't you heard?' The struggles with that impossible English 'H'.

'In Hertford, Hereford, and Hampshire . . .' she sang softly as she got out of the bath and started to comb her wet hair, defiantly dropping every H she could. There were more ants now. They'd reached the ceiling. She could see them in the mirror above the basin as she cleaned her teeth. She spat and gave herself a long, hard look. Bathed, she felt better, not a day over fifteen and could tell herself quite truthfully that she didn't look a day over thirty. But, and it was a big but, there was something uncomfortable about feeling fifteen. The way she did when she was still at Hastings High. She peered closer at her wide, green eyes and caught a flicker of fear.

'Fear of what?' she asked herself out loud. 'How are you going to explain the last twenty years to Bitty? That is if she asks?' Again she answered her own question out loud. One look at Bitty in the drive, hands on hips, shouting at Antonio, and she knew in her heart they'd never have the silly, giggling chats she'd had with the girls at the Maison almost hourly. And they'd never talk about important things that women talk of – love, life. Above all love. Minou was by nature a truthful person and it embarrassed her to tell lies. But one inkling of the truth and Bitty would dismiss her as a tart and start talking about ditches again.

'Tituss . . . Tituss . . .' Bitty stood alone in the drive looking up at the big rock behind the house. The dogs lay around in anxious shapes waiting to be fed while the smell of meat cooking rose from the dog room where three big pots bubbled on a Calor gas cooker. 'Titus . . .' Minou followed Bitty's gaze. It was almost dark, just the tip of the mountain pink in the last seconds of the day. She could just make out a solitary figure dressed in white. It must be Titus. Funny, she'd never known what his name was. Helen, so vague, had never mentioned it. He must have heard his mother, she thought, but gave no answering wave. Bitty turned and strode into the house in her bossy air-hostess walk. Minou wriggled into her briefs, light and lacy as her unshakeable belief that, Bitty or no Bitty, every new day could be wonderful. A couple of mosquitoes zigzagged through the open window. She reached for the Mitsouko and squirted them, then watched the army marching up and down the tiles, wondering guiltily if ants had nostrils.

CHAPTER THREE

THE COPPER POTS shone, the curtains had been newly washed and the old kitchen smelled of mint. The shopping was tidied away into the fridge, the deep freeze in the pantry and cupboards under the sink. Juanita had made a tortilla, the most perfect yellow circle cooling on the table beside a pyramid of oranges she'd piled up in a big blue dish. None of which did anything to dispel Bitty's ill-humour. She slapped the *Sunday Times*, the post, a large envelope and some new flea collars down on the dresser and, without breaking her stride, arrived at the drinks tray. No ice, no lemon, just gin and a splash of tonic. Gibraltar was hell.

'Gibraltar was hell,' she told the Peke since there was no one else around to give a damn what sort of day she'd had. Minou, she noted, hadn't even had the good manners to come downstairs and say hullo. After twenty years. Just left that stupid car for her to move. And as for Titus, well, what could you expect?

'Gibraltar was hell,' she told the Peke again. 'Three hours at the border. Would you believe it? Three hours!' Another strike at the customs, the Spanish side of course, political retaliation, they said – but what for? No one would ever know and, as usual, it was the public who suffered. Trapped, blocked in all directions, she'd jerked along in the herd of hot-roofed cars bashing her horn at the unfairness of it all. Moment by moment her dress getting tighter until she felt it was cutting her in half. She must have put on at least six pounds since leaving the solicitor's office.

'The law is the law, Mrs Nolan.' She mimicked Norman Trail's prissy voice out loud, beyond caring if the family of sweaty tourists in the next car were sniggering at her. 'The law is the law!' No wonder they called him Entrail. Officious idiot! She'd been near to hitting him.

'As I told you last week and the week before, Mrs Nolan, I do sympathise with your predicament.' The hell he did. If he'd had the sense God gave a goat he'd have told her sooner. Given her time to think. But no, he'd waited until the last moment to drop his stink bomb. And, furthermore, Bitty was sure he enjoyed every moment of her dismay.

'So, when Sir Desmond arrives, all that's needed is Miss Latour's signature.'

'Whose signature?' It was a month since he'd said it but even now she still felt sick with shock.

'Miss Latour, your er, half-sister? I take it she is conversant with your intention to sell La Preciosa?'

'Conversant? What's it got to do with her? Nobody's heard from her for twenty years, except my mother, and then only at Christmas. What the hell's it got to do with her?'

'According to your late father's will . . .'

'My late father's what?' No one had said anything about a will. It was a dream, a mad, cruel nightmare and a month on she still hadn't woken from it. Cody had never done a responsible thing in his life. He even died irresponsibly, leaping up to get his fourth Oscar and dropping dead. In front of all those people.

'There must be some mistake.' There had to be. The house was hers. Cody had said so.

'Do what you like with it!' He'd shouted down a very bad line from Kowloon, twenty years ago.

'I have lived in La Preciosa since my son was born. It is my home to do with as I choose, which is to sell it to Sir Desmond Macmahon.' She refused to discuss the matter any further but left the office with terror in her heart.

With Cody there were always mistakes. Minou, for a start. And when she herself was nineteen, he'd got it all wrong then, as well. Tall, with silvery Saxon hair and such a good skin, she'd assumed, without giving it too much thought, that with Cody as her father – she'd be a star. Still she seethed at the memory of that awful lunch at the Savoy.

'Forget it, sweetheart,' said Cody, quite kindly but very firmly. As if he was auditioning just anybody.

'But . . .'

He took her hand across the table. 'Do you want to be a film star or an actress?'

Bitty blundered into the trap. 'A film star, of course.'

He shook his head. 'It isn't in your eyes, sweetie . . . You've got to have it in the eyes.' Her own silly, blue eyes widened with lack of comprehension. But he used lots of quite ugly actresses, that Italian one with the big nose.

'She's not pretty, I grant you,' Cody agreed. 'But she is beautiful. With a flaming intelligence.' Bitty couldn't think what he was talking about. She'd experimented for hours with eye shadow. Everyone in Hastings thought she had very pretty eyes. He tried to make it up by giving her a hundred pounds to buy a pretty dress.

'And how's that little sister of yours?' he asked. Bitty whirled round the revolving doors and almost fell on to the pavement. Minou again. The little by-blow!

She poured herself a second drink. It took the first one for her to realise how tired she was. She sat down at the table, eased her swollen feet out of her sandals and propped her legs on a chair. Another of life's injustices, those legs. Despite the pills everyone was raving about they got more like bolsters every day. Water retention, that's what it was. And stress.

'Oh, Pookums, we were so nearly there, weren't we?' She bent down awkwardly and scooped up the sleeping dog. As a rule things didn't go right for Bitty, but just for once the worm had turned. Literally, because of worms.

The new American neighbours building that hideous villa at Pelayo had dropped in for worm pills for their overfed spaniel. Always in a hurry and always wanting something for nothing. They were on their way, they said, to Jerez, to visit Desmond Macmahon's bodega. The one his family had owned for over two-hundred years. God alone knew how they'd got themselves invited. Clutching the pills, the Americans raced back to the car. Desmond Macmahon was with them.

'Marbella, wasn't it? 1969?' He'd got out of the car and was leaning against it looking out over the terrace. The American wife wanted to be off but Macmahon insisted on staying for a drink. Almost before Bitty offered one.

'Small world, isn't it?' said the American husband. Bitty thanked her lucky stars she'd got some of the Macmahon sherry instead of that cheap stuff tucked away to offer the locals. They sipped their *fino* and talked about the view and the house. How it was the real thing. Bitty told them the pirate story. The Americans, who'd already heard it, oohed and aahed. Titus pretended to be a deaf mute. Desmond said very little very charmingly, except to Titus who addressed him in impeccable Spanish then switched back to very rude sign language and left.

'A very difficult age,' murmured Desmond understandingly to the apologising Bitty and accepted another sherry for old time's sake. She was flattered but bewildered. As far as she could remember they'd never met, that is never actually been introduced. She'd never been in his league. He was friends with the Duchess of Alba. Charles and Diana had stayed with him, of course, when they came to Spain. She'd seen him in the old days, when Nolan was off on business and she went to bullfights with her chums. He was always so elegant, she remembered, dressed as he was now: a lightweight suit, a blue tie and those wonderful English shoes, polished as chestnuts. Desmond enquired about her husband. 'Ex,' said Bitty with a brave smile.

A few days later Desmond rang her. He asked her straight out if she'd be prepared to sell La Preciosa. He was almost diffident, said he knew it was a hell of a nerve as it probably meant so much to her. He offered £300,000. When she recovered her powers of speech she put him at his ease and accepted.

So for a few days life was good for Bitty, who walked around in a glow of triumph. Everyone was trying to sell and no one could. So much so that most people had given up in despair. The Costa del Sol was dead.

Before the buildings had been completed, damp rose and foundations sank. Now they rotted, grey and abandoned. Those who had holiday fincas started off with such enthusiasm and verve, had long since sold for a fraction of their investment and returned to deal with their number one mortgages. The package deals had fallen by fifty per cent, the peseta went nowhere and most of the restaurants and bars stood empty night after night. The sea was toxic and the bonanza was over. Not, of course, that the *bojeo* came under the heading of Costa del Sol, which ended more or less officially just outside.

The *bojeo* was still unviolated. The curious sudden stretch of land covered with cork forests and oleanders had never been built on save for the rare isolated farm. Partly because it was a military zone. A vast radar disc scanned the Straits and it was claimed could tell what Colonel Gadaffi had for breakfast. But the real reason was the levante. The *bojeo* was famous for its view, that spectacular sweep overlooking one of the seven wonders of the world. But it was also famous for being a natural wind tunnel. It drove people mad, that wind; it was said if one committed murder while it blew it only counted as manslaughter. Bitty couldn't believe her luck. She hadn't even tried to sell and then it came, an offer out of the blue. And she could return to England where it rained when it should, where it was green, where the phones worked, where dogs didn't get tics, where there was decent TV every night and where she could read the *Sunday Times* on Sunday. God, for once, was on her side. But not for long. The blow fell fast. Entrail told her that she was not the sole owner of the house. Minou . . .

Minou of all people, a dream slashed in two because of Minou. Of course she didn't believe it and for days refused to accept such a stupid idea. But today Entrail won. In that horrid, stuffy office he'd actually shown her the will.

'... And to my natural daughter, Josephine Marguerite Latour ...' Bitty stared at Cody's flashy signature moving around like a snake, rising from the paper to strangle her. He must have been deranged. That was it! She'd have him certified.

'But Mrs Nolan,' Entrail pointed out reasonably, 'Mr Cody has been deceased for five years.' He went on calmly, '... Who is therefore entitled to half the proceeds resulting from all or any sale of the said Property, Residence, Lands and other Entitlements.' Those being that lot of scrub land up in the Sierra Cabrito which one couldn't do anything with because the military had it.

'Contest the will! Contest it!' shrieked Bitty. Entrail's secretary came in at this point with a cup of tea.

'To contest a will, my dear Mrs Nolan, takes time. It is a costly business with no guarantee of success. Meanwhile, Sir Desmond is most eager to complete and it would be, to say the least, unwise to delay and risk the sale falling through.' Unwise! It would be disaster. All those bills, that great hole in the bank about to be filled up, like cream in a pot, with money, real money. Entrail was talking at her again. He was always droning on at her. Only the other day he'd rung and suggested that he got in touch with Minou himself. The nerve! But she'd rung Helen in Hastings immediately.

'Mummy, where's Minou? No, never mind what for, just track her down. Find her. Fast.' Helen had obliged.

'I take it Miss Latour *has* been informed?' Entrail had said today, rather suspiciously, she thought.

'She's here,' snapped Bitty, which wasn't quite what he'd asked but was true. Josephine Marguerite Latour was singing upstairs in her room. Come to claim her pound of flesh. She *must* know about the house. Why else would she be so idiotically happy?

But think as she might, Bitty couldn't work out how Minou *could* know. She hadn't told a soul, not even Titus. Especially Titus. No, the only people who knew were Desmond, Entrail and the surveyor. The lengths she had gone to for it to remain so had been testing in the extreme. Take the day the surveyor came. Other people got thinner when challenged but she'd blown up like one of those fish who need bulk against predators. She'd managed, got rid of Titus who'd have guessed something was up with a surveyor snooping around. All it took was sparking off a row with him over breakfast and he'd sloped off to Tarifa for the day. She'd been more than gracious in allowing Juanita and Antonio time off to go wailing to yet another funeral.

'Who died?' she'd asked with unaccustomed concern. Juanita told her it was the postman's mother-in-law. Bitty thought fast. Since it wasn't a close relative the most that would be expected was a courtesy show of grief at the church. She asked Juanita where the unfortunate lady was to be laid to rest. Tarifa. Oh, why not Cadiz or Seville or even Algeciras?

'Why don't you take the rest of the day off?' The wretched woman, far from being grateful, just looked at her in astonishment, then said something about mending the curtains for the spare room. But Bitty insisted that such domestic details were unthinkable on such a sad, sad day.

The surveyor had been twenty minutes late. A neat, bald little man without much to say for himself. He went about his business in what Bitty, although thankful, considered rather a perfunctory way. She steadied her nerves with a little quick one in the kitchen but he was done in less than half an hour and caught her on her hands and knees mopping up a stream of water leaking from the fridge. He asked her about contents and looked at the aged fridge.

'What contents?' She thought of offering him a drink but then that might keep him hanging around. He said something about fixtures and fittings.

'Oh, that. Well, everything in here for a start.' She waved her glass at the kitchen and led him into the salon. 'And . . .' She looked round as he took in the dog-desecrated sofas and shredded rugs. 'Oh, the lot!' Yes, the lot, then she could start again, escape those miserably fake ancestors sneering at her from their flaking paint. Think of it. No more cast-offs chosen by some prop man. She could go to Conran's and get new stuff that didn't need to be tucked and turned to hide their stains. Or, better still, Osborne & Little. Yes, she'd let them loose with frills and swags and interlinings. The surveyor started to make a list.

'That is all, except the table and that.' She pointed at the Twelve Apostles sideboard. She could still get a good little price for them. No point in being too impulsive.

'Oh, damn!' The dogs were barking in the drive. She looked at her watch. It could only be Antonio and Juanita back from the funeral. Oh God, she *knew* they'd come back. Bitty bundled the surveyor, still writing, out on to the terrace.

'Yes, yes, the lot . . .' She made a sweeping gesture taking in the pond, the jardinières, the wheelbarrow.

'Everything in the sheds: there's a deep freeze and some ladders. Everything!'

She got him round the front of the house and into his car. If Juanita asked any questions she could say it was someone who'd taken a wrong turning or the new accountant for the dog charity. But she was bound to say something. The Spanish grapevine was even quicker than the ex-pats' small-talk. Before a thought had time to leap into words it was a fully fledged certainty. Details of skeletons long-buried in local memory were disinterred and decorated with rumour. Usually with grudging envy for those on the way up, coloured by the deep hope that sooner or later they'd be down again. And who should know better than she?

'Bitty's open secret' was what they'd called Titus from the start. Of course they'd have said it even if it wasn't true. Word flew just as fast in those days, from party to party, where it was always fiesta: tapas, sherry and olé! The days when she wore flowers in her hair. She knew her bullfighting then. She'd even read *Death in the Afternoon* or most of it. Her cronies thought it terribly romantic. One or two of them had done it. Ava Gardner had done it. Bitty and her bullfighter. Of course it hit the gossip column in Marbella and took less than a week for the rumours to speed off to Nolan, her husband, on a business trip in Helsinki. Titus was born nine months later in the London Clinic. Nolan was not amused.

'They lose all that hair, don't they?' Bitty asked the nurse anxiously as they stared at the child's unexpected mop of black curls. Nolan, as the nurse recalled, was as fair as his wife.

'Sometimes,' she replied with dubious tact.

'Oh, Lord, that's torn it.'

Nolan only came to the clinic once. He stared down

into the crib, his face scarlet and the muscle in his cheek throbbing.

'Isn't he like you?' cooed Bitty, almost without a quaver.

'Oh, come off it Bitty, he'll be shaving by the end of the week.' With that he walked out. He told her he didn't want to see her again. If she got on with the divorce with no hassles and no demands he'd pay an allowance for her and the boy until he was twenty-one. Bitty could never understand why he did that. Probably saving face. Or slapping hers for her one moment of glory in the sun. It never occurred to her that he might just be a very kind man.

She swallowed the third drink and was close on pouring the fourth when Juanita swayed in behind a pile of ironed clothes. The dogs followed and settled at Bitty's feet, gnashing and nipping at their paws and licking their private parts. Juanita told her Antonio had fed them as the Señora must be tired.

'He says the Jack Russell is no hungry.'

Bitty ran a practised hand over its dry nose. Juanita sorted the laundry into piles.

'For Titus.' Her brown hand patted his white shirts in a benediction. Bitty gritted her teeth. The woman spoiled him rotten, always had. Loved him as much as her own, she said, more than hinting that she was some sort of relative. Which well she might be as El Toro was related to most of Algeciras, or so they claimed. Juanita sensed her disapproval and shook her head. A son should love his mother, a mother should love her son.

'The Señora Minou has no washing?'

'She'd hardly arrive with a suitcase of dirty clothes, would she?'

Juanita laboriously posed the question that when

Minou did have need of her services, was it all right for her to do her washing?

'I really don't care.' Bitty was in no mood to be drawn into a discussion about Minou's laundry arrangements which would inevitably lead on to the subject of the new washing-machine; and possibly wages. Juanita, who was about to mention that soon it was the Feria, stopped as Bitty's angry back and empty glass succeeded in warding her off. Not that Juanita disapproved of drinking as such. She'd been born and raised on one of the great vineyards, wine was to life as the sun was to the day. She had six brothers and four sons, all dark, little men who glowered from the tapas bars where passions flew from laughter to sad songs and the occasional fight. But with gin? With gin there was never any laughter for the Señora. Gone was the golden girl Bitty had been when young – long since gone. She'd never been what Juanita would call *mucho inteligente*, but she'd had an open house and open heart. Although she'd stopped short, even then, as if afraid to be discovered performing any little act of kindness. As if in some way it might be construed a weakness to diminish her. Little by little there were fewer people and more dogs. Her anger held no passion, just a lingering bitterness. It was the Gordon's, which Juanita knew brought nothing but darkness and despair.

'The Señora is tired?'

'Four hours at customs. The Spanish side. Of course, I blame . . .' But she couldn't be bothered to battle with the language at this time of day. Juanita should be gone by now, leave her in peace to *think*. Antonio hooted in the drive.

'*Momentito*!' Without haste Juanita crossed the kitchen like a soft black pigeon. She changed her plastic sandals for another identical pair, squashed a crash helmet on her head and leashed it under her chin.

'The tortilla is good. Eat tomorrow – better then.' Antonio hooted again.

'Buenas tardes, Señora. Hasta mañana.' Juanita gathered up two large plastic bags of garbage, one in each hand, and left for her wobbling journey home on the scooter, via the municipal garbage tip.

It was dark now, still no sign of Titus, only the crickets chirping and an occasional grunt from one of the dreaming dogs. The faint strains of 'Where or When' came from the guest room upstairs. Bitty put her head in her hands and groaned. Suppose, just suppose, Minou refused to sign? She had the right to. She even had the right to move in if she wanted. What if Titus leaned on her? What if they ganged up together? She wouldn't put it past either of them. She turned her head away from an insolent letter from Barclaycard and cut herself a large slice of tortilla. She deserved it. At least she'd dealt with the matter of wages. That singing was getting on her nerves. Any moment now she'd shout out for the woman to shut up. With her total being Bitty wished Minou would just vanish, anything. Better still, take up Holy Orders. The Peke farted.

'Oh, Pookums, really.' She let the animal slither to the floor. Her knee bone, she noticed, stuck up like a white dome from its surrounding bib of pink flesh. She straightened out her leg but it looked worse. All wrinkly. She bent her leg again and drew a face on the dome with a Biro. The greyhound slid its elegant head on to her thigh and watched. Bitty's eyes filled with tears.

'What am I going to do with you lot?' It was awful telling the dogs, but they knew it was coming. They'd been keeping very close lately. She cut another slice of tortilla and knelt down to tempt the ailing Jack Russell out from under the table. It turned its head away. It did look very seedy. But it was old and perhaps it was as well if it went on its way now. People thought her callous for putting them down herself. But what else could she do? Spanish vets had moral scruples about birth control and then charged a fortune for putting the poor things out of their misery. The old, the blind, the ones with distemper and those pathetic wretches abandoned on the roadside. Just chucked out of cars when the novelty wore off. And it was getting worse – pedigree dogs these days; the macho, Spanish idea of what a dog should be: boxers, Alsatians, German shepherds, all reduced to skin and bone and brought to her. They could say what they liked but she was the only one who cared. Of course, the Americans and Annie Mason did do a bit of feeble fund-raising from time to time, but it was she who did all the dirty jobs. Like finding homes for ugly puppies, one in ten if she was lucky. Jimmy Fox at the bar did his bit. Not that he'd actually take in a homeless dog, but he did put up some wanted posters.

'Sorry, old girl, this is a bar. In a bar you get rats. With rats you need cats.' He often said that. But he was a good sort, Jimmy, even if he did drink a bit too much. Bitty weaved unsteadily towards the drinks tray on the dresser again. The Jack Russell was wheezing.

'Here, boy, here . . .' It shifted further back into the darkness, its nose between its paws. Poor thing. Well, it wasn't such a bad way to go. One swift jab of Pentathol to make him drowsy, then another and the poor darling would just slip away. But not tonight; she wasn't up to it tonight. She patted the other dogs, then poured another gin and tonic.

'Perhaps Jimmy would take you?' Jimmy had always liked the greyhound. 'Or maybe you? Just one or two,' she pleaded to the absent Jimmy; then remembered again that he was a cat person.

'No cats here, are there, Pookums?' She sat down heavily. 'No cats here, unless you count the one upstairs. Here, puss, puss, puss . . . Here, Minou . . .' A few ears twitched. Bitty giggled and added whiskers to the drawing on her knee.

Titus lingered outside the kitchen door for a moment. It always took time before he felt he could deal with re-entry from the *bojeo* to the battlefront.

'They say there's buried treasure in the garden. Titus used to look everywhere when he was little. So sweet with his little bucket and spade.' Someone, Minou, he supposed, murmured a polite response as Bitty went straight on. 'Gibraltar was hell! Four hours at the customs, four hours!'

'You must be exhausted,' Minou replied and he suspected she'd said it more than once.

'I need food. Where the hell is Titus?' On cue, he sauntered in wearing his dark glasses.

'How many times have I told you not to water those bloody plants with Perrier?' Bitty screamed her greeting.

'They like it.' He pitched the empty plastic bottle into the bin, turned to his new aunt and took off his shades.

'How do you do. Welcome.' He held out his hand and took her measure. She looked wonderful: neat, clean and tiny in white jeans and a T-shirt. He gave her his best smile, the one with a hint of someone who is never fully understood but who has long since ceased to care.

'Titus.' Minou rose from the kitchen table, kissed him on both cheeks and held him at arm's length, studying his face. 'I have a nephew.' He couldn't imagine why this should delight her so.

If there was one thing Minou knew about, it was men. She'd been trained to take them in at a glance. A very nice boy, she decided instantly, despite his astonishing good looks. It amused her that for the first time since Jean Luc she was aware of the gender of another human being. Long legs, a neat bum and a devastating, wide, wide smile. In Paris they'd swarm around him. And in Hastings? Looks like those would be too dangerous to notice. She watched him put a plastic bag down on the dresser and push his dark hair out of his eyes. There was something wrong with those eyes, she thought, a volcano down there somewhere, at odds with his impeccable manners.

'You're late.' Bitty interrupted her scrutiny. Titus almost flounced across the room. Minou raised an eyebrow. He wasn't gay, of that she was absolutely sure and she was never wrong. But why was he putting on this rather silly androgynous act? Why was he pretending? They exchanged small-talk about her journey and he enquired if she had ever been to this part of the world before.

When she replied that she hadn't, Titus asked, 'Do you windsurf?' As he talked he took some tin foil from the dresser drawer and shaped it into a tray and with long fingers divided leaves from the bag into groups which he laid out in straight rows. Minou told him that she'd never windsurfed but had watched them in Biarritz: 'So pretty, so silent – like butterflies on the water.'

'There are lots of beaches further on, beyond Tarifa. La Paloma, that's the windsurfing place. You must see them. I'll take you, if you like.'

'You haven't been near the beach in years.' Bitty felt she'd been overlooked for long enough. 'What on earth would she want to go to a beach for?'

'To have a good time, get a bit of peace and quiet, a break in the sun, a bit of a tan . . .'

'She doesn't need to.' Bitty interrupted rudely. Minou smiled, as if it was a compliment. Titus wondered if she was too innocent, or too stupid to realise that some people were just unspeakably vile.

'Oh, why don't you just die?' he asked his mother wearily, glancing in the mirror and stroking his cheek. 'Maimed,' he murmured to no one in particular, 'maimed for life.'

'There's nothing wrong with your face, you vain little pig!' shouted Bitty, but she looked strangely triumphant.

'You see what I have to put up with?' she demanded of Minou. Minou looked away into the garden. Bitty was ghastly but she had to admit there was no sign of a scar. Titus turned towards the pantry with the tray of leaves.

'You'll get busted,' said Bitty. Minou, who'd been wondering if they were dope as well, walked after him from the kitchen door and glanced into the pantry. Along the whitewashed walls were shelves of neatly labelled jars. Titus brought some dried leaves back into the kitchen with a pestle and mortar and started pounding them.

'It's a lovely moon tonight, it's nearly full,' she remarked. And then bending to look in the mortar she asked, 'What is it?'

'Marsh-marigold, *Caltha palustris*: it's good for rheumatism.' He was flattered by her interest. Maybe she deserved to be shown the grotto. So far she'd passed all his tests. She hadn't commented on his looks, told him he ought to be in movies or looked at him with the heavy expectancy that women often did. Yes, he'd show her the grotto, but not just yet.

'Rheumatism bullshit,' said Bitty, but it came out as 'shullbit'.

'She speaks Hebrew as well,' Titus remarked, still pounding.

'What I want to know is, what are we going to eat?' moaned Bitty. Her dress was killing her. She tried to unzip it and found she had already. What she'd really like to have done was grab the rest of the tortilla, slope off to the salon, read the *Sunday Times* and watch videos.

'Yes, mother, what are we going to eat?' Titus pounded on.

'There's tortilla.' They all glanced at the empty plate. 'I know,' she went on grandly. 'Chops . . . good old English chops. Queued for hours. Gibraltar was hell.' She waved her hand toward the pantry, rose and followed it like Lady Macbeth, as if it knew the way and she didn't. Titus groaned and looked at Minou quietly sipping the white wine. She didn't look as if she minded a bit.

'Here!'

Minou leaped forward and grabbed the platter of chops as Bitty weaved back. The dogs looked thwarted. 'Sit down, Bitty, you had a long day. I'll cook.'

'Thank God,' muttered Titus. Bitty, having relinquished the lamb, sat down again, noticed the drawing on her knee and pulled her skirt over it.

'Have you any rosemary?' It was difficult for Bitty to

decide which was worse, to have Minou rooting around in her cupboards or to do it herself.

'Should be some. Two quid for the *Sunday Times*. It's criminal. I blame . . .' She struggled with the different sections and started to read the Style & Travel section.

Minou flitted round the kitchen quietly preparing dinner. Titus reached for the post, hoping his seed catalogue had arrived from Dundee. Bitty slouched behind the paper. She had to keep an eye on those two. Minou was at it already, same as ever, anything in pants. 'Windsurfers – so pretty . . .' Who did she think she was kidding? She for one hadn't missed those sideways glances shot at Titus. Well, much good it may do her. Others, younger and prettier, had tried with him and where did it get them? No one got anywhere with his sort. Forever looking in mirrors and stroking his cheek. There was some disgusting Greek who'd been a bit like that.

'Dionysus,' she pronounced inaccurately. Titus and Minou had lost track and said nothing. Minou strained the new potatoes. Bitty's eyes tried to narrow but closed completely. She jerked them open with an effort. Titus was unwrapping a parcel. It was a sweater from Helen. Titus smiled. He didn't like sweaters but his grandmother had knitted it and he liked her.

'Mummy's so silly to keep knitting them. I've told her time and time again you never wear them.'

'You didn't have to tell her, did you?' Titus examined the garment, a classic V-neck in pale grey.

'He was always like that,' Bitty confided in Minou. 'Hot child, a very hot child, forever taking off his socks, opening windows and running fevers for no reason.'

'It's cashmere, isn't it?' said Minou, running her hand over it.

'Have it.' Titus thrust it at her.

'Just a minute.' Bitty lunged across the kitchen table and grabbed at it. Minou backed off to the cooker. Titus held the sweater out of his mother's reach.

'Don't be ridiculous. You'd look like an elephant.' He draped it round Minou's shoulders. A nasty silence settled. Titus wondered what would come next. Bitty didn't like silences. Minou removed the sweater and folded it over the back of a chair.

'Do you like David Attenborough?' slurred Bitty as an alternative to passing out. The healthy Jack Russell was licking up the gin she'd spilled in her grab for the sweater. It dragged itself round the kitchen on its bottom. Titus picked it up and flung it through the garden door.

'That thing's got worms.'

At the word worms Bitty burst into extravagant tears. Titus burned with humiliation.

'Oh, for God's sakes. This can't be much fun for Minou!'

Minou didn't seem to mind, though. He couldn't understand how she could rise above such a nightmare and calmly arrange a posy of syringa in a little blue vase. Minou kept breathing in, kept breathing out.

'The moon's nearly full,' she remarked again.

'I will do what I like and say what I like in front of whoever I like,' Bitty addressed Titus, 'and anyway, she's family.' He noticed Minou brighten a little at this inclusion and couldn't for the life of him think why. She was quickly put in her place by Bitty's afterthought.

'And even if she's not, I have the right to do what I want with my own home.'

'With?' said Titus sharply. Bitty looked at the ceiling in a mammoth attempt not to glance at the brown envelope on the table. The one with Cody's final betrayal of responsibility. The insulted Jack Russell crept into the kitchen and cringed beneath the table.

'My poor baby . . . ' Bitty was on all fours following it.

'I can't stand any more of this!' Titus yelled, charged across the kitchen and vanished through the garden door into the night. It was as if a heavy storm had burst above the rooftop.

'Where's he gone?' asked Minou. She put the chops, spinach, potatoes and watercress salad on the table and lit a candle in a bottle.

'Jimmy's, probably.' Bitty backed out from under the table and heaved herself up hanging on to a chair leg. 'Five hours at the customs . . . five bloody hours.' She clutched at her handbag, the brown envelope and the *Sunday Times* and, holding them to her breast, sailed uncertainly towards the salon.

Titus thrashed through the boundary wood, jumped down on to the grass verge of the main road and kept on running. It only took seven minutes to get to Jimmy's via the short-cut and he was going to make in four. Cars flashed past, lorries thundered, but even at full speed he couldn't shake the rage that had taken deep root. Tangled with his anger was humiliation that Minou should have witnessed his mother's full-blown nastiness. He could run forever but never escape being born of the awful woman and some tin-pot hero who probably never had a bath until he was over twenty. He felt a thick guilt too for having abandoned Minou to an evening of Bitty's meanderings in front of the telly. Not that she was that mindless. There was, as he knew only too well, some intent behind that comment of hers,

'I can do what I like with my own home.' He tried to quell the glittering fear that was gaining strength. As he slowed down he thought of turning back to yank Minou away from those sick-making videos that Bitty got in Gibraltar. Reel after reel of messy footage, Nature in its grisly detail, everything copulating, eating, killing. Bitty sitting there, eyes aglow, drunkenly nodding as the commentator smoothed out birth, death and afterbirth. They ate that too. He used to vomit. Now he escaped to the plants. When their days were done they had the grace to disappear gently, no smell, no bones, so clean, sweet and secret.

The yellow lights of El Snitos twinkled in a gappy way. Another bulb had blown but the word Bar was still intact. Which was all that mattered to Jimmy. The El was there, then three gaps, an S, an N, followed by I, T, O, gap S. So El Snitos it was, although the drunken regulars invented impossible anagrams as to what it might have been. It was a shabby place with bad food and good beer. But what it lacked in comfort and cuisine was amply compensated by Jimmy's big-hearted welcome for the ex-pat locals and the few eccentric Spanish who found their way there. Titus slowed down as he turned into the pot-holed drive. Tonight there were only two cars in the car-park: Annie Mason's dusty Rover and an old Peugeot parked up against a mobile home under the eucalyptus trees. The car-park of El Snitos was far from idyllic but a trysting place for a couple of Spanish regulars. The Peugeot shook as he passed it; Bonker and Bonquette were at it again. Annie Mason's boxer bitch stared grimly through the back window of the Rover at flashes of white thigh and buttock. Her head cocked worriedly to one side as she listened to the shameless racket of orgasmic agitation. Titus strolled past with an icy lack of interest. Everyone was quite used to it. Bonker was a large man by Spanish standards, a retired merchant seaman with mighty shoulders, big fists and a zapata moustache. His girlfriend, Bonquette, matched him for size. She had stiff black hair, a red mouth and fierce eyes. She usually wore high heels, a black skirt with a broken zip and lots of gold bracelets. They never sat at the bar. Bonker collected two gins at the beginning of the evening and returned to the ungirded Bonquette in the car. Once in a while they took a breather, Bonker returned to collect refills while Bonquette stalked haughtily to the ladies. At midnight on the dot Bonker returned the empty glasses, paid the bill with dignified silence then roared off back to Algeciras. Everyone had given up on speculating who they were. Some people thought it quite sweet.

Titus prepared the pace of his entrance and strolled down towards Jimmy and Annie Mason who were sitting at the far end of the terrace arguing about the environment and swatting midges.

'*Hola*!' Titus waved at them and turned to the bar for a beer. '*Hola*, Ingrid.' Ingrid was the barmaid, a Swedish student doing a PhD on the Peninsular. She bit her nails and suffered from migraines. Initially Jimmy'd had high hopes. After all, she was blonde; and Swedish. But Ingrid bolted herself into her mobile home every night and spent her time off rattling around mountain villages, taking pictures and looking at wildlife and ruins, in a shaky little Beetle.

'*Hola*, Titus.' Tonight she wore an unbecoming black and yellow striped mini-dress. Her sunburn reached like scarlet gloves up to her elbows as she polished the bar with jerky little dabs and gave Titus what he took to be a look of adoration over her granny specs. If she took them off she wasn't likely to turn into Michelle Pfeiffer but if one examined her feature by feature she wasn't too bad looking. She reminded him of his plants: pale, serious and shy.

'How's the head?' He remembered too late he'd promised he'd bring her some feverfew.

'Not good, I got too much sun.' She gave him his beer and leaned on the bar staring down at her burnt arms. Titus half sat on his stool. It didn't do to encourage her.

'Thanks.' He took his drink and sauntered on to the terrace.

Wisteria tumbled down the trellises between unmatched tables and chairs that Jimmy had painted a violent royal blue with paint left over from his boat. He admitted to having been pissed at the time. When he screeded the floor he'd replaced the furniture too soon and it set hard in the wet cement along with a melée of his footprints.

'At least no one can nick 'em. And they don't wobble. Nothing worse than a wobbling table.' Titus sidestepped a cat and bent to pat a white goat kid that trotted out from the bar.

'Evening, Titus. How's life?' Jimmy beamed at him with affection.

'All right, I suppose.' Titus sat down with them and turned to Annie Mason. Annie Mason was a crony of Bitty's, a thin, sharp woman who wore track suits and was too brown for her age. She took the environment very seriously.

'Just because you won't use recycled, there's no need to go to extremes . . .' She was grumbling about the lavatory paper which, due to financial circumstances, had deteriorated to bits of newspaper hung on string.

'Newspaper is very hygienic,' retorted Jimmy, 'And its true use is for wiping bums.'

'Oh, you are too disgusting.'

'Annie,' interrupted Titus, 'your dog's getting nervous. The Bonkers are at it.' Annie switched away from lavatory paper with exasperation.

'They shouldn't do that in public. You should stop them, Jimmy. She's on heat.'

Jimmy collapsed with laughter. Annie sniffed and drained her gin and tonic.

'What's all this about Bitty selling up, then?' said Jimmy when he recovered. He dropped his bombshell with seeming nonchalance but his bright blue eyes gleamed with curiosity. There was a tight moment of silence. Funny, thought Titus, it's only half-past ten. Annie sat up straight as a broom and stopped worrying about her dog.

'Bitty selling! *Selling?* She never said anything to me. Bitty selling!' she croaked in excitement. Jimmy and Annie both stared at Titus. The goat stared too. It had a bit of Kleenex sticking out of its mouth like a little pink beard. Titus gently removed it, keeping very still. Rumours were as thick as midges on a summer evening at El Snitos.

'Who says so?' he replied at last, casually.

'Heard it in Gib from old Entrail's secretary; nice girl, great tits.'

'Entrail's secretary said what? But who's buying? Oh, she'll never be able to sell that place.' Titus let Annie do the questioning, but before he heard any more he knew it was true. All those little hints and mysteries lurking around recently rushed together into a great ball of certainty in his stomach. So she'd done it. Bitty had dealt her final card of denial. She was selling his home.

'How much is she getting. Who's buying?' Annie hurled questions at him like javelins. She hadn't noticed he was already dying, oblivious of his pain, indecently discussing his burial in front of him.

'Desmond Macmahon made a good offer, apparently,' Jimmy announced with a flourish.

'I knew it!' Annie threw herself back in her chair and banged her fist on the table. 'I knew it. It all makes sense now. The Notario's cousin told my maid that Macmahon was buying up land on the Sierras, up behind the military zone.'

'He can't be, there's no water.'

'The mines, dear, the mines. He's going to start up the mines.' The idea had only just occurred to her but it was as good a story as any. There were supposed to be old mines up there in the mountains, started by the Phoenicians. Or was it the Romans, or the Greeks? History was vague, everyone maintaining the romantic idea but leaving no space between centuries. Moors, Greeks, Romans, Phoenicians, what did it matter? A vague wave towards Tangier covered most of it and everyone agreed that the Alhambra was wonderful. The only person likely to know was Ingrid.

'Romans or Phoenicians?' shouted Jimmy.

'Phoenicians,' called Ingrid from the bar, buzzing around like an anxious wasp. 'The Romans came later.' They turned back to speculation. Jimmy wagered Desmond was starting up a country club, a health hydro or possibly an exclusive golf retreat for Japanese businessmen. Annie rethought mining and came up with darker intent.

'Nuclear waste. That's it, nuclear waste disposal.'

'What's nuclear waste got to do with anything? You can't go dumping nuclear waste all over the *bojeo*, it would be like chucking it around Windsor Park.'

'Money talks,' said Annie darkly. 'It's either that or he's going to dump it in the mines.'

'Maybe he's going to irrigate, more vineyards.' Jimmy's optimistic suggestion was pooh-poohed. Titus listened to them, his teeth clenched as if lack of speech would stop it being true.

'Well, I must go.' Annie rose. Titus got to his feet, sidestepping the goat again which came at him in a butting rush.

'It doesn't bite,' said Annie scathingly. She and Titus had never hit it off. She was there at the house the day the Alsatian bit him – when he was fourteen, when through his blood and tears he saw Bitty wailing not for him but for her dog. It was Annie who took the animal off to La Linea to have it put down and Bitty who rushed around screaming, 'Oh, my God!' too distraught to do anything about the maiming of her child. Although Annie had a strong sympathy with Bitty, her strong British sense of responsibility prevented her from colluding in having the whole thing hushed up. Nevertheless, since that episode she disliked Titus due to her deep belief that 'dogs knew'.

'Bitty home?' she asked as she paid her bill. 'Is your phone on?'

'She's probably passed out by now.'

'Isn't her sister there or something?'

'Don't bother,' said Titus wearily. 'She's probably in bed.'

'Oh.' Annie scurried off towards her car, skirting the approaching Bonker as if he had some bad disease, with the full intention of dialling La Preciosa the moment she reached her villa.

'Wonder how much she's getting for it?' Jimmy drained his drink as Titus sat down again.

Bonker returned the empty glasses to the bar and paid. '*Buenas noches.*'

'*Buenas noches,* old sport.' The darkness swallowed him up and the old Peugeot backed out on to the road. Jimmy looked round the empty little bar. The goat was eating a crisp packet.

'It's getting worse. Only those two tonight. And Annie. The Coca-Cola man's stopped coming. The fridge has packed up. I've had it up to here. Wonder if Macmahon wants a bar?'

Ingrid polished away the last of the glasses and put on a Beatle's CD. Jimmy sighed and reached under his chair for a yachting magazine.

'A dream, a dream. Go where you like, leave when you want, stay if the fancy takes you. I tell you, that's the life.' He mused through the dog-eared pages with an expression of deep yearning. 'Look at her.' He showed Titus a pretty little boat. 'Look at her.' Titus stared at the wisteria above his head. He'd always known there was a big reason for growing those plants. Bitty thought it was dope, the fool. Why should he bother? You only had to walk six paces in Tarifa to get whatever drugs you wanted. Titus disdained such ordinariness. A joint once in a while, more out of politeness or boredom than anything else, child's play. But with *Atropa belladonna* he could fly like an eagle to the land of the spirits, soar away to another world beyond the mediocrity of this one. What other choice was there? Hastings? Take some awful course, teach Spanish, wear a suit? Out of the question. Yes, he decided, he'd kill himself. Or dye his hair blond.

*   *   *

Bitty woke early and swore she'd never drink again. Her head was sweating. As she shifted, the doomed Jack Russell fell on to the space on her damp pillow. Tears filled her eyes as she felt his nose and patted his brown head with only a courageous attempt to lick her hand as a response. He had to go. Kinder. Her heart broke at the thought of those little curled-up paws. She laid him gently at the end of the bed and forced herself to think. Think. That signing must be done. Minou must be made to understand the situation forthwith and that her signature would be no more than a formality. If the woman balked she'd tell her straight that it was a moral obligation. As she made her daily list, she remembered the antique dealer from Jerez. He'd been after the table in the salon for years. Well, there was no point in lugging it back to England and she could do with a bit of cash to keep going for the next week or so. What else?

'And a diet – today.' She grabbed a lump of flesh on her upper arm and pinched it. 'Yes, a diet.'

Sometime later she billowed across the yellow lawn in her housecoat with a set expression and a small brown and white body in her arms. The vultures waddled after her.

'Antonio!' He straightened up from his digging. She handed him the dead dog and a plastic bag. He took it from her without a word and disappeared into the wood with his spade. The vultures changed course and pursued him.

'Shoo, shoo . . . Don't be so horrid. Shoo!' Bitty took a swooping rush to distract them. 'Get him under quick,' she shouted to Antonio and turned back to the house. Looking up, she saw Minou watching from her balcony.

'Did he die in the night?' she called.

'Call it euthanasia,' retorted Bitty. 'One less mouth to feed.' She'd done her grieving in private so she dismissed the subject briskly. Minou thought she looked remarkably cheerful for someone who'd just dispatched a pet.

'What a shame.'

'Can't be sentimental.' Bitty had the air and tone of one who really knew about animals. 'Oh, piss off the lot of you!' She took another run at the thwarted vultures. 'They've got to go, this lot. They're old enough now.' There was a sound of teaspoons clinking on bone china. Juanita was laying breakfast on the terrace.

'Do you want eggs?' Bitty called out. Minou shook her head.

'Oh well, suit yourself, I'm having scrambled. Juanita! *Huevos* scrambled, *uno*!'

Halfway down the stairs Minou remembered she'd left her beach basket in the salon the night before. The salon was to her the sort of room where one should stand straight and walk well. If she ignored the dog baskets, faded sofa covers, flaking paint and the television, it could have been a room straight out of one of Cody's early black-and-white movies. The ones where they fought duels in front of log fires, slashing off the tops of candles with rapiers. As she crossed the large room, barefoot, she could almost hear the crash of overturned chairs and shouts of 'Do your worst, you dog!' She bent down to pick up the discarded bits of *Sunday Times*. The sun, slanting through the iron *rejas*, cast arabesque patterns on the polished floor.

'Breakfast!' commanded Bitty through the softly painted shutters. The beach basket was at the far end of the room beside a bit of furniture obviously made by a mad giant. It had a multitude of drawers, shelves, cupboards and probably had secret panels. The twelve apostles, carved in black oak, stood along the top staring down in distaste at the empty bottle of Gordon's on the drinks tray below, amid the muddle of unpaid bills.

'Breakfast!'

Minou hurried past coats of arms with stern admonishments along the lines of 'Honour before Joy', hung between portraits of understandably mournful ancestors, knights locked into burnished armour with neat beards and sad eyes. The women all looked as well fed as Bitty but their haughty piousness was belied by breasts bursting to escape the weight of pearls and crucifixes. It was difficult to imagine them having been young, shy, barricaded behind the *rejas* from troubadours and temptation.

'The coffee's getting cold!' shouted Bitty as Minou retrieved the basket and brushed away a little trickle of sand, a memento of the last holiday she'd had with Jean Luc. She pushed the memory away by wondering if anyone would mind if she did some flowers. She longed to fill the empty copper bowls with delphiniums, the dark, purple-edged ones that reminded her of an oncoming tropical night. And those walls. It shouldn't take long to whitewash them and maybe they could find another carpet and get rid of those bogus ancestors. She sighed and gently reminded herself that it was none of her business.

'It's such a beautiful room,' she remarked to Bitty as she sat down. 'Cody had style.'

'The props man, my dear. Would you believe it, he had the whole place done up by the props man.' Minou was about to say he'd done a good job but Bitty hadn't finished. 'Typical of Cody. But then, of course, you never really knew him, did you?'

Minou winced. The barbs were out early today. 'I knew him. In a way. But if we'd met on the street he wouldn't have known me.' It was simply stated.

'Exactly.' The sadness of Minou's remark was lost on Bitty. 'Coffee?' She prodded the beach basket with a fat toe. 'Thought that was yours . . . sand all over the place.'

'I'm sorry.' She wondered why she was so meek, why she was apologising. But it was a lovely day, the air clean and warm and she was going to keep it that way. She lit a Gitane. The sharpness of the first puff, a little requiem for Jean Luc.

It was two years now since he'd been blasted to bits in a backstreet in Beirut. They told her he never felt a thing. To her, it was as if he'd splintered into uncountable fragments that surrounded her like gauze. Through this cocoon she could see Madame who broke the news, her back a little straighter than usual, her hand steady and the brandy that she offered. She could see the sadness and the hangdog sympathy of the girls. She could look at things but didn't want to hear them. She drank a lot of tea, watching Cody's old movies on video with the sound turned down. No voice must be allowed to come between her and the whispers of love and encouragement Jean Luc was sending. At first it was easy to summon him at will, as if she'd just called out to him in the next room. But gradually he slipped away, his presence dwindling into darting visits from time to time, leaving her even more alone with great gaps for the pain. There was no body so there was no funeral. But someone organised a memorial service for him at the Madeleine. It was a grand affair for fellow journalists, war correspondents, photographers and editors of all the newspapers. *Paris Match*, the London *Times* and

Independent, *Le Monde*, the *Herald Tribune*, they were all there. Minou didn't want to go. Reluctantly she dressed in the pretty cotton frock she'd worn when they'd met. She stopped short on the steps of the church. Madame, draped from head to toe in deepest black, let her be and went into the cathedral alone. Minou sat on the steps outside and fed the pigeons. When the tearful crowd flowed quietly down the steps after the service ended, Madame, dabbing her eyes, took Minou by the arm.

'*Courage, mon enfant*, he died for his country.'

Minou didn't contradict. But he didn't die for his country. He died because the world was mad.

Minou could smell something sharp, like hospitals. A syringe, a kidney-shaped dish and some cotton wool were tucked, none too discreetly, under her chair. Bitty was going on about the vultures.

'Absolutely wonderful things – nature's dustbins.'

'No, thank you.' Minou refused an offer of toast.

'*Titus no esta aqui*?' Juanita appeared from the kitchen glaring at the empty place she'd set for him. She dumped a plate of Safeway's crumpets on the table.

'No, he's not here. He was an absolute little pig last night and very, very rude.' She looked up at his bedroom window on the eastern arm. The curtains were still drawn. 'Lazy little sod, disgusting behaviour in front of a guest.' She emphasised the word 'guest' and helped herself to a crumpet.

'Solid cellulite but I am going on a diet.' She blew out her cheeks. 'He's impossible that boy, you'd think at his age . . .'

'Oh, I don't know.' Minou felt if she couldn't defend herself from Bitty, at least she could try to defend Titus from such flagrant unfairness. 'He's a sweet boy, very young. Perhaps he misses his father.'

Bitty let out a humourless cackle. 'His father! That's rich. How can you miss someone you've never known?'

'Very much,' said Minou. Bitty stared at her, butter knife poised. The inference was lost on her.

'You do *know*, don't you?' Minou looked confused. 'You must be the only person who doesn't. His father, my dear was . . .' Bitty leaned towards her. Aha, thought Minou, this must be the heart to heart she'd dreaded.

'His father was . . .' Bitty paused for maximum drama. It was a long time since she'd had anyone to tell this story to. 'His father was the greatest mistake of my life. Except for Titus himself, of course. Cost me my marriage, that little episode.' Minou winced for the boy as Bitty spread marmalade on the crumpet with the back of a spoon.

'His father was Manolo Perez!' It was a grand announcement.

'He was Spanish?'

'Well, he was hardly Irish, was he?' She scorned Minou's surprise. 'He was the greatest matador of all time. Well, since Belmonte,' she amended as there were some things about which one had to be accurate. Gratified by Minou's stupefaction, she bit into the crumpet. Oh yes, my dear, it's not only those of us who live in Paris who see life, not by a long chalk. And Manolo Perez was certainly one up on some sleazy acrobat.

'Ah, no wonder,' said Minou softly. That was the missing link, the reason for the turbulence, the volcanic eyes, the melancholy. Oh, how wonderful Titus would look swirling round with a satin cape.

Titus stood well back on Minou's balcony in the shadows of the room. He was out of view of the two women on the terrace below but could hear everything. Not that he was hearing anything new.

'Oh, yes.' Bitty's voice filled the air with her vanities, on and on, and now Minou was captive to the unfolding of his shabby beginnings. He clutched the cashmere sweater. It was now he'd discover if Minou was friend or foe.

'Springtime,' the voice pounded on, 'in Sevilla. The sort of thing that happens once in a lifetime.' She didn't think it necessary to admit she was more than thankful that it had only been the once. A few hours in a hotel suite. A hot, unsatisfactory coupling and a very swift event at that. Which was just as well since the bedroom door was open on to the salon, full of managers, a couple of the great man's brothers, several hangers-on and a priest, would you believe it, a priest! At one point that old black crone of a mother of his burst in and made him drink a bowl of soup. She wasn't offered a thing. Might just as well not have been there. None of them spoke English. The great Manolo, she discovered, couldn't even read. Actually, they were quite nasty. They even laughed when she took a Polaroid of him kneeling in front of his portable altar. Well, perhaps it wasn't the best moment but how would anyone else believe her? Of course, everyone did later. When Titus was born.

'Does Titus ever see him?' asked Minou.

'No. Died in the ring.' Bitty's voice took on a throb of pride. 'Titus was about fourteen. About the same time as the dog episode. He didn't know a thing about Manolo until it was all over. Annie Mason says it's a pity he ever found out.'

'But he had the right to know who his father was.'

'Well, he went very peculiar when he did.'

'Did you tell him?'

'No, someone blabbed at the funeral. You know what they're like down here. He was the local hero. The whole town, the whole country, went into mourning. Well, they would, wouldn't they? Everyone claimed to be a cousin so it was bound to come out sooner or later. They kept kissing him and shaking his hand. And she was the one who told him.' Bitty shot a black look at the kitchen where Juanita was sloshing water on the tiled floor. 'Swears she's his aunt,' she hissed.

'Fourteen,' mused Minou. 'They're so sensitive at that age. It must have been a shock.'

'Yes, but even so, you'd never believe the fuss. He went very odd. He even refused to go back to England to school.' The fees being what they were, this had in fact been a big financial relief, worth putting up with him hanging about most of the time, apart from when he deigned to drop in on the English school in Gib or a little Spanish academy in Algeciras.

'He refused to speak anything but Spanish to anyone, in fact for six months he only spoke to the servants. Everyone said it was because of the accident, you know, when the dog bit him, poor thing.' Minou was aware that she meant the dog. 'But,' continued Bitty, 'to my mind it was sheer bloody-mindedness, believe me. Dramas, sulks, those awful reproachful looks.'

'It must have been a difficult time for him, too.' Minou stuck to her guns.

'Terrible for him? What about *me*? We rushed him to the clinic, he had the best surgeon in Spain, everything money could buy. I even had the dog put down, the best Alsatian I ever had and what thanks? Sheer bloody-mindedness. I suppose it's in the genes. They're a very melodramatic lot, the Spanish, you know.' Titus had heard enough. As he turned into the cool of Minou's room, sudden idiotic tears leaped into his eyes. But he knew what he needed to know about Minou. Gently he kissed the cashmere sweater and laid it out tidily on her bed.

At midday, Jimmy Fox plodded wearily across the dried up lawn carrying a pack of lager, his blue shirt tucked over a neat roll of stomach into a pair of green and orange shorts. The skin around his hairline was bright pink and the nest at his throat was damp. Bitty was storming round on the terrace. The surviving Jack Russell was leaping up and down in a hapless attempt to hump one of the labrador bitches.

'WILL YOU STOP THAT!' The little dog fell on its back with a thump. Minou laughed. Bitty dragged the animal into the kitchen and slammed the door. Then she caught sight of Jimmy.

'Did you shut the gates?' she yelled. 'They're on heat.'

'Walked,' he replied. 'The car's fucked.' He sat down heavily beside Minou and snapped open a can of lager. They introduced themselves.

'You don't look like sisters,' he commented, glancing from one woman to another.

'Different mothers,' snapped Bitty. 'They're all on heat.' She groaned. 'At least any minute now, and I've given away the last of the pills. Why does everything happen at the same time?'

'They say nuns in convents get their periods at the same time,' said Minou, doing a quick edit. The girls in Rue St Supplice quite often synchronised their off days. 'Something to do with the moon.'

'What's the matter with your car?' Jimmy snapped

open another can of lager for Bitty. She took it eagerly. The diet could wait until after lunch.

'It's the gears. Again. I tell you I've had enough. The Coca-Cola man hasn't delivered. The bank manager is having an affair with some bird in Puerto Banús and hasn't been seen for weeks. The fridge has packed up and there's no such thing as a spare part in Europe.' His face crumpled with distress as he turned to Minou. 'It drives you mad down here, mad, we're all trapped and mad.'

'Well, I had to put one of the dogs down.' Bitty interrupted Jimmy's litany of discontent, peeved at not having got hers in first. She flapped her hand at a wasp dying in a pool of melted butter. 'Where's Juanita? She should have cleared this hours ago.'

'So.' Jimmy drained his beer and smacked his lips. 'What's all this about you selling up to Desmond Macmahon, then?'

'What?' Bitty grabbed at a moment to make up her mind whether or not to deny everything. Her expression, she hoped, conveyed astonished innocence.

'Oh, come on, Bitty, it's all over the *bojeo*. What are you getting? You can tell your uncle Jimmy.'

'Bitty, is it true?' Minou asked in dismay. Bitty looked down at her fat fingers. God obviously intended to force her hand.

''Fraid so.' Her voice was charged with sadness. 'Only option.'

'Oh, Bitty, no!' Minou flung her arms open wide to protect La Preciosa and all who sailed in her.

'What does Titus think about it? He looked pretty pissed off last night,' Jimmy told her.

'Titus?' Bitty shot a look at the closed curtains. 'What did he say?'

'Nothing, face blank as snow. But I can tell.'

Bitty groaned. She knew that look, and what it foreshadowed.

'But Bitty, where will you go?' asked Minou. Bitty shrugged as if it didn't matter. There was a frantic whinnying from the salon. The Jack Russell stuck its nose through the *rejas*.

'Oh, shut up! This is the last of the dogs, I tell you. And that goes for you lot, too.' Bitty glared at the vultures.

'Is your phone on?' asked Jimmy, remembering what he'd come for. 'Got to meet a plane, my brother's coming down, got cut off.' Bitty waved her hand towards the kitchen. Jimmy rose, headed off to the kitchen and started shouting at the operator in Spanish.

'Oh, Bitty, what a shame. Do you really have to sell?'

Bitty saw her opening.

'It's not just the money, it's Mummy,' she said in a sombre voice.

'How is Helen?' Minou smiled.

'Not getting any younger. Neither are any of us.' And the morning was gone and she still, for some reason, hadn't got round to this signature thing. It was as if someone clapped a hand over her mouth every time she started to talk about it. It had to mean something.

'Yes, I worry about her. She leaves the gas on. Says she likes the colour. She's quite batty.'

Minou laughed.

'It's not funny. She could blow herself up. She's wandering. Do you know what I caught her doing? Dyeing shoes, dyeing shoes in the kitchen at four o'clock in the morning!'

Minou waited for the rest of the story but there wasn't any.

'What colour?'

'Black,' snapped Bitty vindictively and went off to the kitchen. If Jimmy's brother was coming down the least he could do was bring some birth-control pills for the dogs from that nice vet in Draycott Avenue.

Since she was selling and he was buying it was more than an even guess that the dealer from Jerez would be late. That's the way life was and this near lunchtime it was unlikely he'd turn up for at least a couple of hours. Bitty threw a last morsel of crumpet to the greyhound and went into the salon to inspect the table. What caught her eye was not the deep gleam of dark oak but Minou's purse and a postcard. Obviously, she'd forgotten it when she flounced off to the beach in such a rush. She was still so touchy. She was what she was and it was ridiculous of her to take offence at every little joke. Out of sheer snoopiness she flipped over the postcard to be excluded by the fact that it was in French. This Madame must be a friend, maybe an employer, what? Minou'd never mentioned any man in her life, obviously she wasn't or hadn't been married. Not that Bitty blamed her for that. 'More trouble than it's worth.' Maybe she was a lesbian, after all one never knew these days. Bitty scanned the postcard, absently picking ticks from behind the greyhound's ear. It was then the name sent up a little signal. Minou. She'd signed it Minou, not Josephine Marguerite Latour. Bitty sat down shaking with excitement. The name Josephine Marguerite Latour must be written somewhere. It was all so simple – what did it matter who wrote it?

'I don't want lunch,' she informed the astonished Juanita. 'I'm on a diet and I've got a headache. I think I'll go and lie down for a while.'

Halfway up the stairs she took off her sandals. Her feet made no sound as she walked towards Minou's room. The door was ajar and the faint smell of Mitsouko hung in the air. Bitty noted the cashmere sweater on the bed and the sight of it strengthened her resolve. The drawer of the bedside table was empty save for two hairpins. So it had to be in the wardrobe. There, as she'd anticipated, was a small suitcase beside a pair of high-heeled shoes. With a neat movement she flipped the case on to the bed and unzipped it. Her searching fingers found a leather wallet in one of the compartments, traveller's cheques and a passport. The passport was signed. So were the cheques. Josephine Marguerite Latour. Quite simple, no exaggerated loops or curves, each letter round and distinct. Bitty thrust the passport down the front of her housecoat. There was nothing else of any interest in the wallet, about 10,000 francs in notes, nice to know it was there, just in case. She scarcely glanced at a couple of business cards and the crumpled snapshot. Some man, looked French, bit untidy, arty – no accounting for taste. She replaced the wallet, re-zipped the case and returned it to the wardrobe.

'Shhh,' she hissed at the Peke, swaying down the passage to meet her as she tiptoed out of the room. She swooped it up in her arms and with long, silent strides reached her own room and shut the door.

'Now, be good.' She threw the animal down on the bed where it landed among a bower of pink ribbons on the eiderdown. Bitty cleared the dressing-table of pots, bottles, silver-backed brushes and turned Helen's picture face down. Mummy would think she was being very, very naughty. Sitting at the table she took a long hard look at the signature. There had to be a proper way of doing this. She longed for a gin. No. This was very important. Her list-making pencil was by the phone. Surely one was meant to use tracing paper or something? Juanita would think her mad if she went to the kitchen for some grease proof. Better not risk it and, even better, lock the door. She got up and turned the key then mused along the bookshelf. The complete works of Beatrix Potter on its own wooden shelf, two Jackie Collins which she thought quite good except it was depressing how rich everyone was, *A Dog Lover's Annual* which she'd had since she was nine, *Hymns Ancient and Modern*, a Bible and that was it. That was it! She opened the Bible at the front page and tore out the tissue-like covering off a ferocious Moses, arm raised, parting the seas. He gave her a look. She snapped him shut and sat down at the dressing-table again trying not to think about hissing Schweppes. Upside down? Backwards? With heavy breath and a hard beating heart she tried it both ways, lightly tracing the letters. The start was good until she got to a tricky bit at the end of Latour, a light, upward flick that looked as if it had been written in a hurry or with no interest. The next thing was to scribble on the back then make the impression on a clean bit of paper. For half an hour she laboured until the last attempt was more or less perfect. She tucked it in the Bible and replaced Moses on the shelf. The tell-tale scraps of paper made a nice little bonfire in the ashtray. There was a gentle scratch at the door. Bitty jumped and threw herself down on the bed beside the snoring Peke. It was Juanita wanting to know if she'd like some tea?

'No, thank you,' she managed weakly. 'No, thank you.' Juanita slipped away down the passage.

'Nosy bitch.' Bitty slipped off the bed and unlocked the door with care. One never knew. Titus could be hanging around. Just her luck if she bumped into him. Like a criminal she ran back to Minou's room clutching the passport to her breast as if it might burst into flames or loud music. She anticipated the creaking cupboard, half opened it, slid out the case and replaced the passport where she'd found it. Spine up? Down? Oh what the hell! Back in her room she found she was singing a little tune. She hadn't had such an exciting day for years. With a delicious sense of calm she stroked the Peke's ears and reached for the phone.

'Mr Trail, please . . .'

CHAPTER FOUR

MINOU TURNED OFF the beach track on to the main road and put her foot down hard. It was a long time since anyone had called her black and meant it. She felt as raw as the day when Helen caught her in the bath scrubbing her legs with a pumice stone until they bled.

'Oh, darling,' said Helen, rubbing her with Germoline. 'You must never, ever, do that again.'

And then Jean Luc. The only row she'd ever had with him was when she asked him once, 'Do you mind that I'm not all white?'

He'd slammed out of the apartment and gone to have breakfast in the café. He was deep in *Le Monde* when she joined him. They drank coffee in silence. Then he folded his newspaper, paid the bill and propelled her to the door.

'Now walk,' he said, giving her a little push. 'Walk down the street as if you owned it.' She obliged for a moment, walking jauntily in front of him. Heads turned. Suddenly she thought it funny and hid behind a chestnut tree. They played hide-and-seek along the Seine. And then he kissed her as if there wouldn't ever be a day as happy. She slowed down a bit as her eyes filled with tears. She was hungry, thirsty and disappointed. She lit a cigarette. The hundreds of white windmills stalked along the ridge and were turning fast which meant the wind had changed. Cody would have loved those windmills, she thought, if he'd ever made a surreal version of Don Quixote. She'd thought about Cody a lot as she sat on the beach staring at the breaking sea. She rushed into the bursting waves, rolled in the surf and let it carry her to the shore but still Bitty's barbs were stinging.

'You never really knew him, did you?' Wrong again, Bitty. Minou knew Cody better than anyone alive. In darkened cinemas she'd followed him around the world from the East to the Arctic, France, Italy, China, Ireland. She'd seen every film he made in its original and dubbed into every unlikely language. Each scene, each shot, each frame she could summon at will. It was as if by watching with her soul she could discover what it was he'd meant to Maman and what she'd meant to him. He loved women. Of that she was sure. All his actresses, the old and the ugly as well as the young and beautiful, became goddesses. He knew when he was pushed for time, money, improvising, capturing a magic that had nothing to do with the script. She read the credits to the end, sitting in her seat until the crowds had gone and the cinema was empty, saying quietly and out loud, 'My father made that happen.'

Of course she knew him. Which was more than poor Titus could say about his father. He could have found out everything he wanted but had obviously chosen to obliterate the big fact. She felt a sudden and great sadness for the boy. They both shared such a rickety childhood with fathers to live up to and to live down. But for Titus it must be much more painful, living here, never knowing which pair of dark eyes that glanced at him in a street or café might be an aunt or a cousin. And he, like her, the victim of Bitty's rage for life having failed her. But what could she do about it except run again? To her right Africa rose from the sea. If she were a bird, she thought, she could just fly, drift across the water to her roots. Once, in Paris, a militant black girl had berated her for being so casual about what she was.

'You can never run from your roots . . . You're selling out to white trash.'

Minou replied, quite civilly, that she was perfectly happy sewing sparkles on pretty dresses for rich women and that she'd rather do that than rush about kicking people in protest marches. She could go back to Paris or go to Africa. But Paris was empty now: no Madame, no Jean Luc and the girls all scattered to new lives.

The sudden blast of a klaxon jolted her out of her brooding. A vast juggernaut edged up behind the beach buggy. There was another one in front and nothing but a series of nasty bends for about another four or five kilometres. She peered round the vehicle in front to see if she could overtake it but it was a blind curve. The driver behind her made as if to overtake. Squeezed between the two giants she lost her nerve. She moved in close to the verge and took a left swing up a narrow path. She was annoyed with herself for having panicked but it was pointless arguing with such bulk. A wave of garbage spilled down the hillside, gusts of smoke drifted in and out of smouldering heaps of rotting vegetables dotted with blue plastic bags and water bottles.

'*Merde!*' The rancid smell was overwhelming. She stopped, did a six-point turn, bumping over the remains of a bicycle and, holding her breath, drove at full speed back down the cinder path. The two death-defying juggernauts were gone.

'The wind must have changed again.' She glanced back at the garbage tip and noticed the circling vultures. It was only a couple of kilometres back to the house but she slowed down, reluctant to come upon Titus and Bitty locked into another flaming row. She wished there was a radio in the car. She wanted a coffee. She needed more petrol. She turned into the garage, then remembered that she'd forgotten her purse.

'*Hola,* Minou.' Jimmy Fox was there peering into the engine of his car.

The garage owner wiped his hand on an oily rag and did a lot of shrugging. Jimmy's face was redder than ever, like a small boy about to crumple into tears.

'Is it serious?' she asked as she pulled up along side.

'It will be if I don't make it to Gib to meet the evening plane. What's the time?' Jimmy never knew what the time was. Minou never wore a watch. They both looked at the lowering sun over Tangier.

'Late-ish,' they agreed.

'Can I drive you?' she offered.

'I say, would you?'

'Of course.' That would delay the return to La Preciosa for at least another couple of hours. 'But I need gas and I haven't any money.'

This, to Jimmy, was a perfectly understandable predicament. He paid for the petrol, retrieved a pack of lager from his own car and hopped in beside her. Minou shot off in top gear.

As they sped through Algeciras she listened with half an ear to Jimmy's stories.

'He's a nice chap, my brother Tom, but a bit too

serious for his own good. Gets fussed about being on time and things like that.'

'Don't worry, we'll be there.' They were now speeding along the motorway to La Linea.

Jimmy relaxed and told her about how he'd played cricket for England in Hong Kong, until the airport came into view.

'*Eh, voilà*!' exclaimed Minou. There was only a small queue at the border. Jimmy put his leg over the side of the beach buggy and jumped out.

'Not much point in your coming in. Park just beyond the taxis and I'll nip in and get him.'

'I have to stop here, anyway. I don't have my passport.'

'Oh, Christ!' Jimmy smacked his forehead. 'Neither have I.'

Tom waited for Jimmy at the exit of the airport as they'd arranged. There was no sign of Jimmy. He put down his fishing gear and duffel bag and partly retreated behind the *Independent*. Sometimes people recognised him which he found excruciatingly embarrassing. He watched as tour operators gathered up their pasty flocks, amazed at how much luggage the average British family needed for two weeks in the sun. Spanish taxi-drivers held up bits of card with oddly spelled Anglo-Saxon names but there wasn't anything remotely resembling Fox. It was only a hundred yards or so to the border. The customs shed had emptied which was just as well since if they did ask him to open up there was no way to explain two hundred contraceptive pills for dogs. He was tempted to jump in a cab but the likelihood of finding a bar called Snitos somewhere near Tarifa was remote. He strolled back to the airport exit. An official appeared from nowhere.

'You can't leave that there, sir,' he said, pointing at the duffel bag at Tom's feet. Tom took off his jacket and finished rolling up his sleeves before he replied.

'Is this the only exit?'

'Yes, sir.'

'Is there anywhere I can leave this stuff?'

'Sorry, sir, no left luggage. Security.'

'Beware of false gods,' Tom warned him and was about to enlarge on the theme of nothing is as it seems but changed his mind. He'd opened his big mouth quite enough for one day. He picked up his belongings. Across the road he'd spotted a café on the roof of Safeway's. If Jimmy wasn't already there knocking back one for the road he could at least have a drink himself. He needed one. It wasn't every day you lost your job, your girlfriend and your home.

He chose a table with a good vantage over the airport entrance and ordered a beer. He had a slight headache and suddenly felt very tired. He adjusted his watch to Spanish time. Another lifetime since he'd let himself into his echoing flat in Shepherd's Bush and made straight for the video. Apart from the rumpled bed he'd dragged himself from at 4 a.m. and a change of clothes, the video and the TV were the only things not neatly packed away in cardboard cartons. He wrenched off his tie and flicked the rewind button. He always checked the morning show, just a cursory, professional check. Amanda, his girlfriend, or as he supposed his now ex-girlfriend, couldn't understand his casual attitude to his own image. She recorded, labelled and stored every second of his screen time. She said it was for posterity but he suspected it was for children she expected him to father, which, he supposed, boiled down to the same thing. He wondered if she'd recorded that morning's fiasco but doubted it. They'd had a very brittle farewell sometime in the earlier hours. It would be a pity though if she hadn't. It might have given her some satisfaction to see him make a certain entry into the archives of thundering blunders. Cool Cat Tom blows it!

He had changed into jeans and a sweater, opened a can of beer he'd got in for the removal men and sat down on a rolled carpet to view the worst. For a start he'd looked awful. Make-up, for him, was usually a pretty perfunctory affair but today it had taken three layers to blanch out the shadows under his eyes. The make-up girl who'd seen it all before was appalled.

'Skin like a crocodile . . . hope it was worth it.' She was a nice girl with gentle hands and had a slight crush on him. She was one of the very few who realised how nervous he was before a performance. Even after nine years of television his stomach still refused to unwind until the show was under way. But last night had been enough to unnerve the strongest. Amanda announced, quite calmly but with an underlying note of hysteria, that it was time for serious commitment. Didn't he realise, she said, that it was time? Didn't he realise, she pleaded, that by moving into a two-bedroomed flat he had an unconscious desire to deepen his domestic bonds? This was a new one. He told her that, in all sincerity, he was moving because of the word processor and he needed a study. This didn't wash with Amanda. She told him he was afraid of commitment. He wouldn't have used the word commitment. As far as he was concerned one was only committed to lunatic asylums or prison. Still, he told her, nice try. They argued the old why, why not game until the early hours. She sat on the stacked up furniture looking pale and drinking Nescafé as he told her again and again that she was too good for him, that she had her whole life in front of her; as he'd told Deborah, two Carolines and a Vanessa. Amanda looked sad and said something about a mid-life crisis. Since she was only twenty-three he supposed she must mean him.

The make-up girl ran her hands through his thick, well cut, dark hair and looked at her handiwork in the mirror.

'You'll do, but don't make a habit of it or you'll lose your fans.'

'You're the only one I've got, love.' He meant it but it wasn't true. He had quite a large fan-mail from middle-aged housewives which he ignored. He wasn't handsome. He had at best, he thought, the face of a friendly, intelligent horse. But it was an honest face with straightforward searching eyes. He pulled off the make-up sheet, tied his tie and asked the make-up girl what she thought of it.

'What do you think?' She didn't have time to say as the production assistant popped her head round the door.

'Tom, are you ready? We've got Macmahon, last moment, something to do with Green issues. There's been a shuffle, must fly . . .' She gave him a bit of paper and fled. Tom sat down again in front of the mirror.

'Is this tie all right?'

'It's a bit . . .' She was right, it was awful. Silver, salmon-pink and orange.

'Find me another – dark, black.' With Desmond Macmahon on the programme he needed everything on his side.

They ran the previous night's news for him. A city banquet item with a senior minister making a touching speech about the environment. Whatever Bill Clinton had going for him as a warm-up for increased tax was worth giving a tentative try. He sounded like a nanny, with shades of Mrs Thatcher's scolding intonations creeping in, berating those present, and the nation at large, as if they were naughty children littering the planet with sweet papers. The minister went on, how we, as a nation, were obliged to lead Europe, nay, the entire world, if not the universe out of its despair. Tom kept his eyes on Desmond Macmahon, who was sitting at the top table listening seriously. The platitudinous waffle went on and on. The mystery to Tom was why was Desmond there and in such a prominent position? He was not a public man. It was rumoured that he paid a PR firm a hefty fee to keep his name out of the news. Very few knew how often he had been on the unpublished dinner lists of Number 10 in Margaret's day and probably still was. He'd never held any official political office and very seldom gave interviews. Tom had in fact interviewed him once, some years before in one of Desmond's rare appearances at a Tory Party Conference. No one knew for sure why he was there. Tom was given the job finding out. But he was younger then and greener and probed a bit too far too fast. Desmond, although charming, swatted him as if he were no more than a little insect. Tom, recalling the incident, picked up the phone to research.

'Anything new on Macmahon?' The girl said she was looking.

'Nothing much, nothing you can't get from *Who's Who*.'

Father, an Irish Peer. Mother a de Beer. Educated Eton, Oxford then a stint in the Guards. Inherited the title in 1957. Married a wealthy Stuart girl (deceased).

No children to cause embarrassment by marrying pop stars or getting done for drugs. Chairman of Macmahon sherry empire, established in the early 1700s. Merchant banks, shipping lines, mining interests in Canada and Bolivia. Loaded, in fact. A patron of the arts, National Gallery, the Louvre and Prado. Residences: Galway, Chester Square and the Provincia de Cadiz. Hobbies: none listed. Sex life: in Tom's opinion, highly unlikely. He couldn't pinpoint why it was he loathed Desmond Macmahon. He was no worse than many he'd interviewed and it certainly wasn't because of their differing political opinions. He wouldn't have a job if he'd ever let that interfere with an interview. Not that he had many political opinions left. Fanciful as it might be, Tom had reached the conclusion that the fate of man lay in the hands of a very small group of faceless men. They probably met in a schloss in Bavaria once a year and were, for the most part, bald. You could sit around in clubland for a lifetime and never catch a whisper of who they were. That was if you cared. Somewhere in his mind lurked the idea that Desmond Macmahon was probably one of these men. But why the feeling of unease about him? Maybe it was the blandness of the disguise that couldn't quite hide the blue unchanging eyes, eyes without mercy. If someone had told him Desmond Macmahon was an alien he'd have been relieved.

'I've got Macmahon' he said as he took his place beside Rowena, his co-presenter. She was neat, pretty and as sharp as a knife.

'Rather you than me,' she said, adjusting an earring. Out of the corner of his eye he saw that Desmond had arrived and was chatting amiably with the producer. Other than vague instructions on Green issues he had no idea what he was going to ask the man, and what did it matter anyway? He'd say exactly what he wanted, they all did. His head was splitting and he felt as if he was watching a film from which a great chunk of the plot had been removed.

The empty sitting-room seemed to spin around him as he gazed in disbelief at himself mispronouncing Punsalmaaging Orchibad, the name of the President of Mongolia. Then he looked almost dithery when there was a temporary loss of sound from Cardiff. He was thankful he'd ducked interviewing an actress hyping a book on self-discovery through childbirth and beetroot juice. A wry old journalist dealt with what the papers had to say, which wasn't much. Then in a daze, he watched himself interviewing a fanatical young woman hell bent on the UK shunning anything to do with Europe unless Spain gave up bullfighting. She was fat, rude and stupid. Nevertheless he made a note to link her Spanish comments with Desmond. Then the traffic and the weather. Tom pressed the fast-forward and leaned towards the screen.

The interview started one up to Desmond. The make-up girl and wardrobe had failed him. Desmond gave Tom's tie a kindly look. Tom shuddered. The tie was a disaster. He must have been mad or blind. He turned up the sound on Desmond's series of predetermined statements. To all but the most naïve it was obvious that Desmond Macmahon was at the forefront of the new entrepreneurs: The Clean-Up Boys. Create nuclear waste then clean it up. A piece of cake.

'Is it true that . . .?' Tom made it sound like genuine curiosity rather than interrogation but he was too late. Desmond cut off the imprecise question with a raised hand.

'Every era brings its own hazards, of course it does.'

Tom watched himself lose concentration and struggle to regain it.

'So what you're saying, Sir Desmond . . .' But Desmond was way ahead, off again, referring to 'something the young lady said earlier'. It was now a matter of global importance for the entire human race to gather themselves into a caring community. Which was not what the young lady before had said. She only meant animals. But caring, Desmond informed Tom, was more than an abstract concept. Tom felt a time-bomb of disgust ticking in his head as Desmond rolled on without bothering to masquerade with answers to Tom's irritating interruptions. Tom glimpsed Rowena's eyebrows arched in sympathetic disbelief. All the man had done was buy screen time. It was nothing new. They all did it. Week after week they rolled up giving lip-service of concern to issues that marked only personal advancement and profit.

'But, Sir Desmond, is this not what the *Ecologist* has been saying for twenty years? Didn't Edward Goldsmith bring these very issues into the light in his 'Blueprint for Survival' only to be dismissed as a scaremongering clown?'

'There is to be, and indeed there must be, an inspired collective endeavour and one starts by cleaning out the cupboards—'

'But at the Rio conference the Government—'

'The British Government are to inaugurate a world-wide appeal to benefit the planet . . .'

At this point Tom was off camera. He remembered dimly that he'd started to laugh. They both knew what was happening. Desmond was informing the public, in the most gracious way, that they could pay for the privilege of allowing him to make yet another fortune out of toxic waste. Shipping lines, land, mines. It was insultingly obvious.

'Is it true that . . .?' As he spoke Tom felt hysteria rising then suddenly his amusement was replaced with an overwhelming sleepiness that slid over his head like a paper bag. 'Sir Desmond . . .' He made a desperate effort to keep awake. The lights were blazing hot and he was sweating. 'Sir Desmond—' Tom took his time '—what aspect of this suffering planet distresses you most? That is, on a personal level?' Most of these backstage bastards shied off the word personal. Desmond stiffened; Tom noted it. Desmond unbelievably started to talk about the plight of the seals. As he watched, Tom crushed the beer can between his hands.

Maybe it was because the camera operator was inexperienced, or maybe just bloody-minded, but the camera stayed on Tom. He was watching Desmond as if he'd just discovered something unpleasant in his cornflakes. At the time he didn't realise he'd taken leave of his senses but he obviously had. He watched aghast as his own image said: 'Bullshit!' and then his own yawn. An enormous mouth-stretching yawn packed with nine years of listening to lies, subterfuges, manipulations, cover-ups, self-promotions and every little greed known to mankind. The sound even picked up a little giggle from Rowena. The camera flashed quickly back to Desmond. He had murder in his blue eyes. There was a terse order from the producer to roll up. Before Tom had time to issue a little thanks to Sir Desmond for being with them, the news girl was on again. He remembered Desmond remarking, quite lightly, that he was a foolish young man. He remembered Rowena asking him if he was all right. He remembered the buzzing in his head and decided not to go to the canteen for breakfast because he couldn't stop laughing. He remembered explaining to someone that he had to be with his solicitor by ten to sign the lease of his new flat and he remembered hearing someone say, 'Heads will roll'.

Tom flicked off the set. The flat was very quiet. He'd stopped laughing. Desmond wasn't the sort of man to wait to take someone out to lunch to get what he wanted so it should only take about a quarter of an hour for the Director to ring. He'd run the programme, ask if Tom was in the building, then call. Tom let the phone ring six times before he picked up the receiver.

'Macmahon's been on.' The Director came straight to the point. 'And others. You certainly put your foot in your mouth. You'd better come in and see me.'

'Why?' said Tom.

'You know damn well why. I've enough on my plate without a senior presenter making an ass of himself. What the hell got into you? And don't say stress. You ought to be able to conduct a simple interview without me being inundated with calls from the Cabinet at nine o'clock in the morning.'

'I see.'

'I hope you do.' The Director sounded more exasperated than angry. 'They've got me by the shorts, Tom. You know we're on slippery ground already with Corporation policies. He's hissing for a public apology from you or the boot.'

'I'm not apologising to anyone.' The defiant, lonely words bounced off the bare walls.

'Well, I've got to do something about you.'

'The union won't like it.' That was a trump card and he knew the Director knew it. The Director groaned.

The last thing he needed was any more publicity about anti-government, or for that matter pro-government, attitudes. It was also the last thing Tom wanted. Suddenly the only thing that mattered was to get away and do some fishing.

'You have contravened several clauses relevant to modes of behaviour and you know it.' It was thin but the Director took a gamble on Tom not wanting to stir up a hornet's nest. Tom heard himself agree meekly but with a lurch of excitement. The Director was continuing.

'Suspension for six months and think yourself lucky you haven't got the chop.'

'Shall I work out the week?' He had another three days to go and had just remembered he'd left a tweed jacket in his dressing-room which might come in handy if he went fishing.

'No. Call it what you like, nervous exhaustion, ME, a brainstorm . . .'

'Mid-life crisis?' It was meant to be a helpful suggestion.

'Suspension, a sabbatical – and no bleating to the Press!' The Director hung up with a roar. Tom grinned at the ghastly tie which was dangling from his fishing gear. He wouldn't have to wear a tie for six months. The phone rang again. He was whistling as he answered it. It had to be Amanda. But it wasn't. It was the estate agent.

'Mr Fox?' The man sounded nervous. 'Mr Fox, I'm afraid I've got some rather bad news.'

'They've backed out?' guessed Tom. 'But they can't . . . we've exchanged contacts.'

'Completed,' corrected the estate agent. 'No they can't back out, neither can you. But I'm afraid we've lost Holland Park. They've decided not to sell. I hoped your solicitor would have been in touch with you by now.'

For a split second Tom wondered if Desmond Macmahon had anything to do with it. He lit a cigarette.

'But the removal men are coming in half an hour.'

'I'm terribly sorry, Mr Fox, there's nothing I can say. I've done everything I can to move them.' The young man sounded near to tears.

'What about my deposit? Isn't there a clause, a forfeit or something?'

'They say they are more than happy to let you have your deposit back and compensation for any inconvenience.'

They both hung up. Tom rang his solicitor, who confirmed what the estate agent had said. The doorbell rang. It was the removal men.

'Hold everything.' Tom let them in and dashed back to the phone.

'Maybe it's something in the stars?' deduced his sister in Hay-on-Wye. She tended to go in for that sort of thing. For once Tom didn't scoff.

'I was wondering if I could come down for a few days. Get in a bit of fishing and think about what comes next.' The removal men bumped past him with his bed.

'Oh, Tom, you're more than welcome but the kids have got mumps. You've never had it. Wouldn't be wise.' He agreed. He had no intention of adding his balls to his list of losses.

'Look,' she suggested, 'why don't you send your stuff here? We can store it in one of the barns, it's quite dry. No rats. Cheer up, at least you're not stuck with a mortgage you can't pay.' His sister was deeply practical as well as kind. 'Why don't you go and see Jimmy? He goes fishing. It would do you good.'

'Not quite the same.' Straining after tuna with Jimmy was not quite the same as sitting on a leafy river bank in Wales.

'Don't sulk, Tom. Jimmy's on good form. I got a card from him last week.'

'What does he *want*?' The pair of them had already bailed Jimmy out of a nightclub on a Greek Island and a failing cinema in Hong Kong and put their feet down over a safari park in Turkey.

'He didn't want anything. Why don't you go? He's got a boat, or he's getting a boat or something.'

Tom apologised for snapping at her. 'What's his number?' His sister searched around for it.

'Hang on, there's another one for messages as his phone doesn't always work.'

'So what else is new?'

'Oh, Tom, don't be like that. Here's his address. At least I think it's his address. Must dash, love, crisis in the sick-bay.'

The gas, the electricity and the phone were all paid up. The first-time buyers were about to move in within the hour. Tom tried Jimmy's number and asked for an STD. The operator said there was no such number. He gave her the second one. She said it was out of order. He tried Jimmy's number and got a sound he'd never heard before. He rang British Airways and asked about tickets to Gibraltar that afternoon. He tried the second number and got the engaged tone. The removal men recalculated the cost of taking his stuff to Hay-on-Wye. A blackbird hopped across the garden. He'd enjoyed laying the York stone. Hadn't had much time for plants or anything but luckily the neighbours had some rampant green stuff that trailed over his wall. He hoped the young couple wouldn't cut it back. He tried the second number again. While he waited he looked around the flat with a slight sentiment of regret. The first home, where he'd hung the hunting prints his father had given him, not because he liked them but because they seemed appropriate to a bachelor flat. As his confidence in his own taste grew he'd picked up bits and pieces from the Portobello Road. Although he yearned for a stark, Zen look which in part he'd achieved by painting everything white and plonking a bronze Buddha on the floor by the window, the effect was somewhat marred by the jumble of magazines, newspapers, fishing tackle and discarded clothes which seemed to creep in.

An hour later, still near the airport and unsoothed by the local beer, Tom marched angrily through the empty customs shed without giving a thought to the contraceptive pills.

'For dogs!' Jimmy had shouted, for someone whose name he didn't catch on the very bad line. Once across the border he looked round. Still no sign of Jimmy. A taxi-driver urged him towards his cab.

'Mr Fox, isn't it? Can I have your autograph for my granny?' A hand landed on his shoulder. Tom spun round. It was Jimmy, lager in hand, beaming like the sun at noon.

'Thought I'd missed you, old chap, sorry about that. Forgot my passport.'

The two men stood for a moment giving each other affectionate little pats on the shoulder, both talking at once. It was a long time since they'd been together. Two years, maybe three? Jimmy's happiness swept away any ill-humour and reproofs. But, Tom remembered, Jimmy was like that. He always got away with things by simply refusing to feel guilty. They strolled towards the waiting beach buggy talking about a bottle of Champagne to celebrate.

Minou had got out and was leaning on the bonnet smoking a cigarette. She'd taken off her espadrilles and still wore only her sarong.

'Minou, this is my little brother Tom. Not so little, eh?' Jimmy glanced up at Tom with pride.

Tom, slightly startled by this shoeless woman who appeared to be wearing nothing more than a small tablecloth, nodded and shook hands. Jimmy's taste in women had improved. Or maybe not. Jimmy gave a long sigh of lust at the sight of two overweight girls whose T-shirts declared they came from Wolverhampton.

'Come on, come on, a man could die of thirst here.'

Jimmy climbed in the back with the duffel bag and fishing gear. Tom sat in the front beside Minou, hoping she was going to put some shoes on before she started up.

'How long can you stay?'

'Indefinitely,' Tom admitted.

'Lost your ratings?'

'In a way. Packed it in for a while. How's the fishing?'

'Not bad, not bad at all. Boat needs a bit of fixing, though.'

Minou kept her eyes on the road, half listening to the two men, Tom giving Jimmy news about their parents, their sister and friends. Jimmy responded with the woes and wildness of running a bar in the sun. She was surprised at how different they were for brothers, but their ease and friendship lifted her spirits. This was how it should be, not like the awful atmosphere at La Preciosa. She shoved the thought away and slowed down at a roundabout. On their left the oil refinery blazed into the sky and the high-rise flats of Algeciras were spiking up ahead of them. Tom looked depressed.

'No escaping it, is there?'

'Costa del Horrifico. It's worse up the coast: Arabs, gangsters, Benetton and kiss-me-quick. Welcome to sunny Spain.'

Jimmy enlarged on the demise of the coastline and sighed for the time when a beer cost what a beer should cost. Minou noticed Tom was holding fast to the handrail. He was probably one of those men who mistrusted women drivers. A sentiment, she'd learned, not confined to Englishmen. She hadn't missed the worried look he'd given her bare toes. Nothing obvious, but Minou felt things about men fast. It was an instinct she'd had most of her life which had nothing to do with St Supplice. She had a flame and she'd wasted it, sending out sparkling invitations without a thought. But that was before Jean Luc. She was wiser now and good wine, she knew, should be reserved. But with the best intentions, eyes and feelings well under control, in some mysterious way, her hands, shoulders and slim knees seemed to send out invitations that any French, Italian, Spanish or for that matter Portuguese would recognise. Acknowledge and pursue, or not, according to opportunity or inclination. But Englishmen weren't like that. Tom had not addressed a word to her. Yes, Englishmen functioned differently, if and when they did. The girls often commented on it. It seemed they had some deep unconscious battle with senses taught early by cool mothers, bossy nannies and distant fathers. When they were very young, she knew they were incarcerated in old, grey buildings to which they formed deep attachments. Those institutions may have built characters and empires but any show of emotion was deeply discouraged. Save for the scoring of a goal. That could provoke a good old shout or the singing of the school anthem at the end of term could bring a lump to the throat. Anything else was regarded as a perilous outburst. Tom, still clutching the handrail, responded as best he could to Jimmy's banter, but Minou felt the city smoke and tiredness around him despite the clean blue shirt.

'Did you have a good flight?' she asked. He looked surprised that she spoke English. Perhaps he thought she was Spanish. She remembered that Jimmy, in his excitement, had forgotten to introduce her.

'Haven't quite arrived yet,' admitted Tom. She smiled.

'Champagne, Champagne, that'll bring you into focus,' cried Jimmy joyfully. 'Let's stop off at the Yacht Club.'

'Yacht Club?' Tom sounded alarmed. 'Am I all right?'

'It's not that sort of place. Relax, don't take it all so seriously.'

'It's sometimes better to be serious. It makes less important things more important.' Minou smiled to herself again. It was the sort of thing Jean Luc might have said when he was very tired.

'If it makes Champagne important, be as serious as you like, take a left here.'

They were through the town and reached the traffic lights by the bridge. On the far side of the road was a sign with 'Algeciras Yacht Club' in pale paint. Minou stuck out her arm and cut across a truck full of Spanish soldiers to go exactly where she wanted to be. She flashed them her widest smile and took one hand off the wheel to blow a kiss. Tom clutched the handrail again.

As soon as they entered the bar Tom relaxed. Jimmy was right. It certainly wasn't that kind of place. It could have doubled for almost any station buffet in the Midlands, save for one window shaped like a porthole and a lithograph of a galleon in serious trouble sometime in the late nineteenth century. Jimmy ordered Champagne.

'Welcome to Spain.' Minou and Jimmy toasted Tom's arrival. 'Now let's have a look at the boat. Needs a bit of fixing.' Jimmy led the way through the bar to the quayside.

It was a matter of opinion as to whether the *Darrack* would last the night. The little fishing-boat was listing badly in the greenish water. The cabin door hung by one hinge, streams of rust marked the dull blue sides and a shoal of toxic fish swam freely through a hole in the hull. The only signs of better days were a pair of faded tartan socks, some pink briefs on a washing-line and an old Stilton pot full of clothes-pegs.

'Ah,' said Jimmy fondly. 'She was a stout-hearted one.'

'What else is wrong with it?' asked Tom, trying to swallow his disappointment as the fishing trip vanished.

'Off the top of my head I'd say the bilge pump's cracked, the motor's on the blink and it would cost a fortune to caulk the hull. But with a lick of paint . . .'

'Not worth the mooring fee,' pronounced Tom. 'The kindest thing to do is scuttle her.' They all stared at the *Darrack* in silence. Jimmy refilled the glasses.

'To days gone by and days to come. Come and

see what I've found. A bargain, a dream. Going for a song . . .'

Tom closed his ears. When Jimmy said bargain it was best to run for it.

'Isn't it getting late?'

'What for? You're in Spain now.'

They walked three abreast along the quay past lines of pretty yachts bobbing gently against each other in the dying light.

'There she is!' Jimmy pointed with the Champagne bottle.

'Oh, look!' cried Minou, 'Look, it's so pretty!'

Reluctantly Tom glanced across to the far side of the harbour. He had to admit the *Dancing Lady* was the sleekest thing he'd ever seen.

'What is it?' asked Minou. 'A sailboat or a motorboat? It's got a mast.'

Jimmy beamed at Minou for asking intelligent questions and addressed his sales pitch to Tom.

'Got everything. Cruising speed ten knots, new prop shaft and bearings, three lavs.' The two men walked ahead of Minou towards the boat. 'Perfection, flush toilets,' he added over his shoulder for Minou's benefit. 'Mainsail's by Ratsey, so you know what you're getting.'

'Who's getting?' asked Tom nervously.

'Radar, automatic pilot, built at Wisbech.' Jimmy was unstoppable.

'How much?' Tom could have bitten off his tongue.

'It belonged to a Texan, oil tycoon or something, shacked up with a drum majorette. She's only nineteen. He died on the job. Well, if you've gotta go, you've gotta go. She's dropped right down from 165 to 130 . . .'

'130 what?' asked Tom sarcastically.

'Don't be like that, man. Look at her! Think of it, sell the bar, get a bridging loan and off to the Laccadive.'

Minou sipped her drink and gazed at the *Dancing Lady* scarcely moving in the still water. She felt a surge of affection for Jimmy almost hopping from one foot to another, so excited, so ready to try again.

'To where?'

'The Laccadive. It's the new place. No one knows about it yet. Paradise. Makes Bora-Bora look like Blackpool and I tell you it's finished here.'

'Where is it, the Laccadive?' Minou asked, not really caring. What did it matter where paradise was?

'Somewhere near Java.' Jimmy waved the Champagne vaguely in the direction of the sea. The two men faced each other, Jimmy bursting with his dream, Tom nervous and serious listening to talk of cruising speeds and prop shafts. Minou half sat on a stone bollard. Little spots of light from portholes twinkled in the water and the smell of tar gusted her to evenings in Forte de France when Maman held her hand as she took her evening stroll along the waterfront. When daylight died in the Caribbean an orchestra played waltzes in the café where Maman swayed among her friends showing off the pretty dresses she made in her boutique. From the café they could see the tall masts against the orange sky. Those were big black ships with rust red sails. These were neat, small and domestic. People lived on them doing purposeful things with bits of rope. Just below her a girl was peeling vegetables.

'Hullo there!' A voice broke the peace. A woman in a green track suit strode along the quay, dragging a boxer on a plaited leather lead. Jimmy broke off.

'Oh Lord, it's Annie Mason. Not a word, not a word,' he commanded.

'What are you lot doing here?' shouted Annie, who was on her way to have drinks with a retired Rear Admiral. Jimmy dodged the question by introducing Tom and Minou. Minou leaned forward to shake hands, not noticing the approach of a young woman, laden with groceries, being dragged along by an eager standard poodle.

'Look out!' shrieked Annie as the poodle hurled itself between them towards the boxer bitch. Minou, drink held high, leaned back and put her hand on the bollard to steady herself. But it wasn't there. Her glass flew from her hand and landed with a tinkling crash on the deck of a boat twenty feet below. The girl peeling vegetables let out a cry as Minou, arms curved into a graceful back dive, fell towards the scummy water. Minou was aware of praying she wouldn't be crushed between boats. Tom leaped and grabbed. She felt two bands of iron round her ankles. Instinctively she pushed herself away from the slimy harbour wall, only inches from her head, as Tom hauled her up like a bucket from a well. He held her high until her hands could touch the quayside then gently let her down in a heap. There was a lot of laughter and barking.

'Lucky you had your knickers on,' said Jimmy.

Annie shouted insults at the girl with the poodle. Minou righted herself, the blood flowing back to its normal place. She rubbed the white impression Tom's big hands had left on her ankles.

'I hope I didn't hurt you,' he said, 'but I didn't know if you could swim.'

'I can, but thanks all the same.' She got to her feet slowly. Jimmy offered her more Champagne but she refused. She was trying to remember something. Something to do with sound.

'You sure you're all right?'

'Absolutely, absolutely.' Then it came to her. The sound was the safe sound. The slap of his hands on her ankles was the same sound made by the catcher in the circus.

CHAPTER FIVE

'EVERYONE OFF TO the beach, then?' urged Bitty, sipping her lemon tea. Juanita said the weather would change by lunchtime.

'Nonsense.' The sky was clear and blue but the weather forecast was pessimistic. Minou finished her coffee thinking about the beach. Tom's handclasp had turned into two muddy blue bruises round her ankles and her legs ached a bit. Bitty watched her wavering.

'It'll be beautiful on the Tarifa side,' she urged, although she couldn't for the life of her understand anyone's need to get wet and covered in sand. Like most residents Bitty could truthfully say she hadn't been near a beach for at least three years except to give the dogs their Christmas Day run.

'Here, my darlings, look what Mummy's got for you. Nice man brought pilly willys from London.' The dogs lumbered over to her. 'No, not for you, old boy.' She gave the three bitches their pills and stroked their throats to help them down.

'So, it's off to the beach, then. Titus, what about you?' Titus was deep in *Hola!* magazine. Bitty gritted her teeth. Just revving up, that was it, the faraway look, the silences, sudden little appearances in doorways, the turn on the heel, the quick vanish. Oh, she'd seen it all before but this one promised to be the biggest storm ever. But she could take it. By the time they came to carry away the furniture he'd have to say something, do something.

'Would you like to go to the beach, Titus?' Minou picked up her basket and stubbed out her cigarette.

'Got things to do,' he murmured.

'Well, you'd better get a move on.' Entrail's secretary was arriving at midday. Bitty started to sweat. She hadn't had a drink for twenty-four hours and had eaten only three bananas since the night before.

'Don't you feel well?' Minou asked, noticing her sudden pallor. 'Would you like me to stay?'

'No, no, no. You're here to have a rest, enjoy yourself.' In her effort not to scream it came out at best unlovingly. 'Don't worry about me, it's just withdrawal.' Bitty had a foul taste in her mouth, and come to think of it, she did feel a bit faint. Nerves, that's what it was.

'The first three days are always the worst. The tummy shrinks and it's not so bad.' Bitty gave Minou's flat stomach a black look, quickly overlaid with a weak smile. Oh, if only the woman would go. There just wasn't time today.

'Anything I can get you in town?' Minou walked slowly to the door, not quite limping but taking it carefully. Bitty appeared to think for a minute, staring thoughtfully out of the window.

'Well, since you ask, there is something. The birds, they've got to go.'

'Birds!' gasped Minou following her gaze to the black huddle on the lawn. 'What birds?'

'The vultures, of course.' Minou sat down again quickly. 'Oh, come on, all you've go to do is find the right place and they'll do the rest. Antonio will put them in boxes or something. Just open the boxes and they'll do the rest.'

Bitty called Antonio through the open window and gave some very precise instructions in quite good Spanish and turned back to Minou, too appalled to think straight and make a rush for the beach buggy.

'Yes, there's a perfect place just off the main road three kilometres after the Bolonia turning, take a left after the restaurant, head up the hill for another ten kilometres. I've got a map if you like.'

Minou stared at her helplessly, the instructions unheard. She had to touch those awful things, feel those scraggy necks in her hands. Suppose they bit?

'Well, you did ask,' said Bitty reproachfully. Titus threw down a magazine and stood up.

'You really take the cake.' He gave Bitty his best withering look. 'It's OK, Minou, I'll come with you.'

'Oh, would you?'

'Well, get on with it then.' Bitty glanced at the kitchen clock out of the corner of her eye.

Antonio was standing by the beach buggy with a cardboard carton tied with string. It wasn't very big.

'Are they all in there?' Minou shook the box. It wasn't very big and was very still.

'Si, Señora, one, two, three,' said Antonio in English and proudly held up three fingers and put the carton in the back of the buggy.

'Would you like to drive?' Minou held out the keys but Titus was already in the passenger seat.

'No thanks.'

'Are you sure?'

'He doesn't,' revealed Bitty, who stood under the fig tree tapping her foot. 'Get a move on, the weather might change.' She waved them on. Minou thought it would be nice if she just managed to say thank you.

'Have a good time. Why don't you take each other out to lunch? I'll just nibble my lettuce leaf. I'll be a wraith by the time you get back.'

'Fat hope,' muttered Titus.

'Why are they so quiet?' They'd gone about half a mile and the box in the back was sinisterly still. 'What do they do anyway, quack?'

'Hiss.' Titus turned and jiggled the box. The string was quite loose.

'Don't, they might get out.' Minou crouched over the wheel to put as much distance as she could between herself and her passengers.

'Take a right here,' instructed Titus as they reached the garbage tip.

'But it's too soon, Bitty said—'

'Take a right.'

Minou pulled off the road and started up the cinder path towards the steaming mass of rubble on the top of the hill. The box jumped about as she bumped over the half bicycle. She wanted to hold her nose but kept on driving with her breath held as the putrefying stink invaded the buggy. Glancing up she saw a few black shapes wheeling high above the tip. When they reached the top Titus told her to turn the buggy around.

'Keep the engine running.'

She swung round in a half circle and came to a halt facing downhill. Titus grabbed the carton from the back seat and jumped out. Minou kept her hand on the brake. Titus vanished then reappeared in the gritty smoke of the bonfire the council hoped would eventually dispose of trash strewn three hundred yards in every direction. He tore away the cardboard and struggled with a great bundle of feathers. Antonio had not only tied their feet but tied all three together. A gust of rotting vegetables rose on a little wind, and cinders flew up around the windscreen. Still high, the circling wild vultures watched as Titus shook the three birds out of their box.

'Quick, step on it!' He ran back to the car and leaped in. Minou revved the engine and took a quick look back. The three vultures stood where he'd dumped them looking stupid.

'Quick!' Minou let out the clutch and drove at full, jerking speed down the cinder path, feeling she was about to be pursued by demonic forces. Once on the main road they both broke into helpless giggles.

'What about lunch?' said Titus. 'I'm starving.'

Entrail's secretary was due at any moment. Under the circumstances Bitty had offered to pay for a taxi but Entrail said the girl had her own car. Bitty wondered what the world was coming to. She'd put on a navy skirt and striped blouse, all too tight of course, but it didn't look holidayish. Strains of 'Guantanamera' drifted from the kitchen. Juanita was in a good mood. She'd been paid – in cash. The dealer from Jerez had stumped up quite a good price for the table. Of course it was probably worth double but sellers can't be choosers. The ice was in the bucket, gin and tonic at the ready. Bitty wandered towards it, steeled herself and made do with a Ritz cracker and an olive. It was tough. Eyes shut, she let a wave of joy rush through her. By this evening all her troubles would be over. Well, the end of the week, as it would take a day or two for Desmond's cheque to clear. Not that there would be any problem with a cheque from Desmond Macmahon.

'Steady, old girl, we're not there yet.' Bitty walked from the fireplace to the window and back again, then looked at her watch. This diet business was a nightmare.

'Antonio!' she summoned. She needed him close at hand. She went into the kitchen where Juanita was stitching a mountain of carnation-red net. A Feria dress for her granddaughter. Bitty was about to comment on the extravagance then realised she didn't give a damn what the woman did with her money.

'Juanita, tell Antonio to mend the shutter in the downstairs loo. If this wind keeps up we'll be awake all night.' Back in the salon she flipped open the *Sunday Times Magazine* in an attempt to steady her racing mind. There was an article about Desmond, of all people. Obviously an omen. He stood foursquare beside a sundial in the rose garden of his house in Wiltshire. Oh, Wiltshire, how wonderful, all warm and mellow, nestling in a proper English afternoon. She stared at the picture thoughtfully. He wore tweeds. What a handsome man he was. Funny that he'd never remarried. But then neither had she. The only difference being that he must have had a choice. Turning this over in her mind, she wandered over to the drinks tray again. Perhaps just a teeny, weeny sherry, some of the Macmahon sherry of course, just for luck. Such a gentleman, yes, gentleman, that was the only word for it, so polite without being slimy or dramatic like the Spanish. The way he remembered everything, like the Queen. '1969, wasn't it?' he'd said, so she must have made some impression on him. Maybe, when she'd shed a few more pounds, she'd invite him to dinner. No, lunch. Lunch was less obvious. Just to show him the ropes, of course, and then they could talk about old times. She denied herself the sherry and even another olive, vowing she'd lose a stone in a week even if it did mean taking some of the herbal diuretic stuff Titus went on about.

Entrail's secretary, Mona, arrived in her neat little Metro at exactly midday. A pretty girl, if a little on the heavy side, but even with her briefcase she'd have failed an audition for a yuppie. It was the white high-heeled shoes that let her down.

'How do you do?' Bitty held out her hand. 'Would you like a drink? A sherry? Or perhaps something stronger?'

Mona said no thank you, although she had every intention of joining Jimmy for a few once she'd finished at La Preciosa. She sat down and opened her briefcase.

'Such a shame about your sister, glandular fever, isn't it? My auntie had it.' Mona produced a sheaf of papers.

'Oh, she's over the worst. I looked in on her a moment ago, awake but only just. I said I wouldn't bother her with coming downstairs. I'll just slip up to her room and she'll sign.' Bitty held her breath in case Mona had any legal objections but she hadn't.

'That'll be fine. It's just these few. She must sign here, here and here.' She indicated some pencilled crosses on the papers. Bitty all but grabbed them from her.

'I won't be a moment, just make yourself at home.' Thankfully, Antonio was banging away in the downstairs loo. Bitty paused in the doorway to enjoy the moment to the full. Of course she was an actress, a wonderful actress, a natural. Lady Macbeth would have been a piece of cake compared to this. In a way she wished she'd worn her red velvet housecoat. So much for Cody and his 'You've got to have it in the eyes' rubbish.

Josephine Marguerite Latour: the three imprints came out perfectly. Oh, the joy of it. Bitty took her time, sauntering back from her room to the salon with the tell-tale tissue paper in her pocket, scrunched into a tiny ball.

'Is it all right if Antonio and Juanita are the witnesses?' she asked Mona lightly. 'They can read and write.'

Blonde Mona scarcely looked up from the Christmas edition of *Vogue*. It wasn't every day one got out of the office. As far as she was concerned that fat Peke could sign.

'Oh, that'll be fine.' Meanwhile, she thought, I think I will have a drink. She got up and helped herself to a gin and tonic.

CHAPTER SIX

A SMALL GROUP of old men in dark suits sat on the low stone wall either side of the narrow path leading into the old part of Tarifa. Some of them were limbless, some sightless and most toothless. They gave no sign of noticing the locals, the tourists or the windsurfers save for the shift of a pipe or walking stick. Their silent presence seemed to imply a password was necessary before entry to the small town was granted. Titus led Minou under a moss-stained stone arch and down a very steep cobbled street, one of several running parallel. He acknowledged the guttural greetings of '*Hola,* Titus' from the bakery, the tabac and the gloom of small bars with a quick wave and kept on walking, so tall, so regal. It occurred again to Minou how odd it must be for him. That each one should know who and what he was, but he, uncertain if it was a distant cousin or an aunt who passed him on the street or watched from behind lace curtains on the first floors of the thick, stone houses.

'Cocaa, haaash, smack . . .' A gaunt youth with blazing eyes sidled up to her, selling in a rushed hiss. Titus dismissed him with a sharp word and he slithered like a shadow up an alley. The Street of the Little Parrots, the Avenue of the Evening Star, the Plaza of the Lady of the Light. The names delighted her. Each little street was just a narrow alley overhung with wrought-iron balconies, a handshake away from each other. Here and there a thick, black door stood open on to the secret life of the courtyards, the flare of geraniums, soft ferns in terracotta pots and a woman stringing up white washing.

'This is one of the sights.' Titus stood aside to let her enter the fish-market. 'It's been here for ages, since the Romans, probably before.' Under a glass roof supported by twelve stone pillars, stout housewives in black cardigans and plastic shoes ambled past with kilos of tomatoes, onions and green fans of bananas. The end of the hall echoed with shouts, the crash of wooden boxes and the slap of wet fish. Red tuna, raw as uncooked ham, cockles, squid, mullet and green lobsters. A tiny, toothless lady in a white cap screeched as her sprays of glittering sardines flew from scales into plastic bags and large bluish plaice dripped into the marble gully. Minou gasped at the size of a decapitated head of a swordfish, its eyes staring at her like anguished buttons. The old lady shook with laughter and slit open another belly.

'This way.' Titus strode out of the market, down another thin street, then turned left and right several times.

'There's no local hero, unless you count him.' They were passing a statue of Guzman the Good. He glowered beneath a neatly crimped fringe, his down-turned mouth almost hidden by a fine walrus moustache. He leaned on his broadsword as if he'd slipped a disc.

'What did he do?'

'No idea.' They turned another corner and Minou stopped in front of a bullfight poster.

'Is he a local hero?' She pointed at the matador. Titus gave her a sharp look.

'I suppose so. They all are.'

'Bitty told me about your father,' she said gently.

'Of course she did. It was no secret to anyone except me.'

'It must have been a shock.'

'Not really, it was rather funny.'

'Funny?'

'Hilarious. Can you imagine: "Who is my father?" And I almost had to shake it out of her. "I was so young", she kept saying, "I was so young".'

'Well, she was.'

'Twenty-six if she was a day. She got rather cross and seemed to think it was my fault.'

'Oh, Titus.' Minou linked her arm through his and hoped he wouldn't flinch away. 'I bet there aren't many people who had perfect beginnings.' She was glad he smiled.

The main square wasn't really a square, just a broader street in the depth of the town with a few tourist shops and a couple of discos. It was here, he told her, at the Café Central, that everything happened. The Central, though very unremarkable, was full, tables taken either by more old men who evidently lived there, big blond Germans writing postcards and groups of slim, sleek suntanned French girls.

'Damn.' Heads turned and the girls stared as he asked the waiter for a table.

'About half an hour. Would you like to see the church?'

She hadn't the heart to tell him that churches weren't usually on her agenda. It was at the end of the street: large, baroque, but not big enough to be called a cathedral. Two white pigeons perched picturesquely on the outstretched arm of Jesus and she thought how tactful they were not to sit on his head. A few of the girls at St Supplice went to mass quite regularly and she'd tried it once or twice. Neither she nor Bitty had any formal religious instruction other than divinity at school and carols at Christmas. What little she'd discovered about it for herself had given her to believe it was there primarily to make one feel bad, inadequate and wrong. But had anyone accused her of being an atheist she would have been quite shocked. She knew there was a rhythm somewhere, a pulse in the spinning universe and that if one listened carefully enough it told one what to do. But gods, if there were any, didn't live in buildings. In the blue gloom of the interior a few old ladies sat on wooden seats staring wearily at the main altar. A few more, white hair covered with black lace, knelt in rheumatic supplication. Titus and Minou walked quietly up the side aisle past an anguished Christ which she found morbid. She hoped Titus wasn't offended by her lack of enthusiasm.

'Awful, isn't it?' he admitted, looking up like an angel at the gilded ceiling and fat, floating cherubs. 'Juanita used to drag me in here when I was small. She wanted to save my soul, I think. She still does.'

They stood in front of a Madonna simpering above a forest of dripping candles. Minou's sense of style was outraged. The Madonna wore a blue dress which she knew to be appropriate, but surely those who held these things sacred could have done better than polyester. She told him Juanita was far more her idea of a Madonna and he agreed.

'Well, that's enough of that,' Titus said with relief

and turned towards the shaft of light beaming from the street.

Outside she remembered Madame's postcard.

'I need a stamp.' They walked close against the wall to avoid a lorry in the middle of the road. They were slinging fairy lights up from one side to the other outside the Post Office.

'It's the Feria soon.' To prove him right a loudspeaker test blasted an incomprehensible jabber, a few bars of a tinny *paso doble* then a crackle and cut off. Titus waited outside while she bought her stamp.

'Your boyfriend?' he questioned as she slid the card into the letter-box. Minou smiled and shook her head.

'It's to a lady I used to work for in Paris.' If he should ask her about her work, she'd already decided, she would tell him the truth. But instead he asked if she'd ever been married.

'Bitty's never really said much about you.' Except, as he remembered, short, bitchy dismissals if Minou's name cropped up.

'No, I've never been married. Not in the technical sense.'

Titus waited for more. She had been loved. A love without that little trick of ownership. But maybe that was because Jean Luc had always been away at some war. The church had depressed her and she couldn't talk about Jean Luc today. She closed the subject down with a sweep of her eyelashes. Titus respected her reluctance and in silence they climbed a steep flight of stone steps. At the top he asked her: 'But you are French, aren't you?' She stopped to catch her breath. Her ankles hurt a bit.

'I suppose so. That is, I was French until I was seven, then I was English, then I was French again and now,

I don't really know.' She sounded as if it really didn't matter.

'Bit like me.'

They climbed another flight of the steps leading into a small square. In the centre was a fountain, mosaic-lined and surrounded by palms and oleanders. The houses round the square were large, standing wide and apart. Some had Moorish grilles over the windows and one had an onion-shaped dome. Although the tops of the palms swayed against the bright sky, where they stood was sheltered and very hot.

'This is the posh bit, the mayor lives up here and that's the town hall.' Minou sat on the edge of the fountain and ran her fingers through the splashing water.

'It's full of surprises, this place.'

'Yes, isn't it.' His voice had a sarcastic edge as he pointed the toe of his boot at a hypodermic under an oleander and a couple of used condoms stuck to the side of a stone bench.

'There's a word in Spanish,' he told her, 'taken from the word Tarifa. "Tarifada" – it means crazy. I expect it's the wind.' He beckoned her to follow him up a long slope on to what turned out to be the ramparts of an old fortress. They walked right to the edge. The wind blew their hair back from their faces. Across the water Tangier was just a soft blur and Jebel Moussa had vanished.

'Levante,' shouted Titus. The waves in the harbour were white-capped. It wasn't much of a harbour, just a derelict tanker and a few fishermen spreading acid green nets by their shabby boats. Here and there earth-diggers jerked aimlessly back and forth between piles of loose rock and rusty anchors. A car drove along the quayside and stopped by one of the fishing-boats. She thought she recognised it as Jimmy's.

'Let's have lunch.' They turned back to the town, pushed by the force of the wind. Minou pointed at a banging 'For Sale' notice on the door of a little windowless house.

'What a wonderful address. First on the left, on the Mediterranean.'

'Or last on the right. Depends which way you're going.' But the levante whipped away his words as he pointed back towards the heaving Atlantic.

He persuaded her to have caracoles.

'What are they?'

'Tiny snails. They grow on the tall grass and in the hedgerows. Very local, very Spanish, very piquant. I'll see if they've got any.' He went inside the café. It was the flat, quiet time of afternoon and the Central had emptied except for two of the old men and those who had only pensions to go to when the beach was wild. Across the road a woman locked up the laundry. Her windows were hung up to the ceiling with dresses for the Feria: white, red, green, with layers of braid-trimmed heavy frills around the hem.

A man in a blue shirt and jeans walked slowly along the far side of the road. It was Tom Fox. Minou sipped her beer and watched him, surprised that she hadn't immediately recognised him as being English. He had an ease about him, when believing himself unobserved, and moved as if he was comfortable with his body but his head, slightly hung, was troubled with his thoughts. She wondered if he was coming to the café, but he stopped and looked warily in a windsurfing shop. Titus came back, sat down and offered her a cigarette. Two French girls conferred with giggles, nods and nudges. One of them came over and asked him for a match. He stood to light her cigarette, wordlessly, politely, sat down again and slumped into his chair with a scowl.

'What's the matter?' She was taken by surprise by his swift change of mood. 'What comes next, Titus?' She leaned forward and touched his sleeve with the tip of her fingernail.

'Dunno,' he said almost inaudibly, then blurted out, 'Bitty's mad, she never thinks! She just rages, all these vague rages of hers blundering around in her head finding their way out of her mouth. Even the dogs think she's crackers. It's got a name, you know,' he said earnestly. 'Cognitive dissonance.'

Minou's English failed her. 'Cog—'

'The complete inability to recognise any facts, however obvious, which conflict with her view, no matter how ridiculous.'

'Selling the house?'

'Yes.' His face had turned the colour of cement and she suspected a sudden glint of tears.

'Have you any plans?'

'Nope. Nothing much to do around here.' There was a painful hush. One of the old men at the next table threw a bit of a roll to a sparrow. A car turned into the deserted street. With a shake of his hand the man warned the birds. It flew up as the car passed and with aching difficulty the old man rose, bent, picked up the bread and tenderly crumbled it for the bird, which flew back and started pecking again.

'What about England?' Minou asked.

'Nothing much there either. I can't go back, Minou, back to kippers, porridge, Hastings or some awful tidy village in Wiltshire.' He was desperate for her to understand. 'You see, down here it's different. It's a feeling I can't explain, it's the people. They know who they are. They don't in England.'

'Then why don't you stay here? Haven't you any friends?'

'A few, but sooner or later someone makes a remark. If you look like I do these people *expect* something.'

'No one wants to be what they are, not really,' she told him. 'The trouble is, they don't really have any idea of what they'd rather be.' As she said it her voice seemed to echo in her head with the idea but she knew he'd understand, as if their frail beginnings joined them in a club of the unclassifiable.

'You see . . .' she went on but broke off as a shadow fell across the table. It was Tom Fox.

She introduced Titus as her nephew, amused to see Tom's transparently disapproving assumption that he was her toy-boy change with an almost over-friendly handshake.

'Titus was at school in England,' she added just to reassure him even more. Tom asked him where. Titus responded briefly and retreated into a minor sulk. Tom declined lunch but ordered coffee. He glanced down at Minou's white espadrilles.

'How are your ankles?'

'Fine, thank you.'

Titus called for the waiter and ordered himself a brandy in rapid Spanish. He rather overdid the Andalusian slur.

'Would you like one?' Minou asked Tom.

'No thanks, I've got to get back with the car. Jimmy wants it to take another look at the *Dancing Lady*. He's managed to get the keys.'

'Good for him,' muttered Titus, and finished his brandy in one gulp. Tom rose.

'I only came into town to see if I could set up a bit of fishing. But no luck. Everything seems to be shut. Must be siesta. Haven't got used to this place yet.'

'The table's gone.' Titus's voice echoed round the salon. The far end of the long bare stretch of polished floor was marked with six dark rings where the sturdy oak legs had stood all his life. 'It's started.' The shutters banged, the clouds hung low, the garden had turned into a furious, swaying wind tunnel and the vultures were back, huddled against their wall.

'Oh, *merde*.' The thought of another row was exhausting. 'Do you think she knows yet? She'll be furious.'

'Furious? She's always furious.' Titus was still staring at the space. They moved about the room in silence, Minou picking up magazines and the copper that had been dumped on the floor. The dogs lay around looking accusing.

'You mean furious like the other night?'

'That wasn't furious, that was just a quiet evening at home.'

Although it was muggy Minou felt cold. She needed light and movement. She piled more logs on the waiting fire and looked round for a match. The phone shrilled in the kitchen and went on shrilling.

'She must be out. Juanita doesn't answer, doesn't believe in it.'

Titus went into the kitchen, Minou followed to find some matches. Juanita was sitting at the table surrounded by more piles of red net.

'*Donde esta la Señora?*' Titus asked her. Juanita bit off a piece of cotton and turned to the window to re-thread her needle. She told him Bitty had gone out to lunch just after the Señorita had left.

'The vultures are back,' she told him with a chuckle. Minou picked up the tiny adult dress, scattered with red polka dots. Titus answered the phone and said 'yes' a couple of times and then his jaw went rigid. Juanita glanced at him with a worried frown.

'You can speak to her yourself, she's right here.' He handed the phone to Minou. 'It's for you.'

'Me? It can't be. Who is it?' She let the little dress fall on to the table.

'Norman Trail. He's a solicitor.'

'Solicitor?' She took the receiver cautiously but with the full knowledge that there was a mistake.

'Hullo . . .'

Titus leaned up against the dresser watching her as Entrail launched into apologies, telling her how deeply sorry he was that his secretary had been so remiss. That it was good of her to have signed the documents today when she was so unfortunately indisposed. How, much to his embarrassment, his secretary had neglected to include all the papers and that there were two more in need of her signature. Minou listened intently, as if it were a soundtrack being played backwards. Norman Trail was a man used to having his say before listening. If he could presume upon her for just one more moment, he wanted to impress upon her, as he was sure Mrs Nolan had, that Sir Desmond was anxious to take possession as soon as possible. And lastly, since completion was in sight, into which bank would she like him to pay the cheque? As for the signing, he would send the girl at her convenience? Some deep instinct warned Minou to keep her mouth shut.

'Thank you,' she murmured, as he wished her a speedy recovery.

She stared at the bowl of oranges. Her bones had

turned to powdered glass. Juanita asked her if she'd like a cup of tea.

'What did he want?' Titus looked as strained as she.

'There must be some mistake.' Her voice was thin and she felt as if there were insects buzzing round her head. 'He said he was sorry to bother me when I was so ill, but I'm not ill. I didn't sign anything. And, and where would I like him to pay in the cheque. *What* cheque?'

'Have you signed anything? Has Bitty got you to sign anything?'

'No.'

'Who was here today?' Titus turned on Juanita. She pulled a tacking thread from a frill.

'*Es bonito*?'

'*Si Juanita, muy bonito.*' Titus dismissed the tiny dress with a wave of his hand. 'Juanita, who was here today?' He wished he sounded a bit more like Colombo or at least had a dirty mac. That way he could deal with the spear of excitement that made him feel so thin and taut.

'Was anyone here today?' No one, she told him, except her and Antonio and the Señorita from Gibraltar. We signed the papers, she told him proudly, me and Antonio, as *testigo*; she should have worn her black and maybe a flower, the way she did when she went to vote for the mayor. Minou, sitting at the kitchen table rolling an orange from one hand to the other, listened as intently as Titus and suddenly discovered she'd understood every word of Spanish the woman had spoken.

'But what did they witness?'

'I've a pretty good idea. But I don't know why or how.'

Juanita knew that voice and the expression in his eye.

She crossed herself and thrust her sewing into a carrier bag. Quicker than she'd moved since the big fire on the hill, she changed her shoes and went out to find Antonio.

'The levante is bad at the full moon,' she warned, coming back for her cardigan. 'Bad moon this time, black moon,' she muttered and went out again to wait for the scooter in the drive.

Low, gun-metal clouds rolled in from Africa. The French windows were wide open, curtains whirling to the ceiling, their pretty blue dulled down to a dirty grey. One of the labradors was asleep by Minou's bed. It gave her a look and waddled out as she struggled to shut the windows and was thrown back into the room by the force of the wind. After battling for what seemed an endless time she secured the catch. The curtains fell back into place and she threw herself on the bed. The room whirled round with her thoughts as she went over and over what Titus had explained. That in some way Bitty couldn't sell the house without her signature. Which must mean, Titus had concluded, that she must be a beneficiary. She felt sick. It was the caracoles. She leaned over the lavatory and closed her eyes against the yellow slime spurting up from her stomach. Her head sweated and her hands were cold. Half crawling back to the bed she noticed the cashmere sweater, clutched it round herself and fell back against the pillows. Minou struggled with horror of the sour taste in her mouth, the wind, the banging shutters, each little nuisance blown up into a gigantic assault, as big a force as Bitty's hatred. No longer could she sweep away that terrifying dislike as she'd dismissed the ugly sniggers in the locker room at school. She clutched the sweater, trying to bring back

Helen, so watchful then, so seemingly uninvolved but always there to smooth away her little gust of despair. Those clouded, half-rememberings tangled with the bitterness of the moment. Cody had remembered her. And no one had ever told her. She knew he'd died broke. Everyone knew that. All he'd had was the house and left half of it to her. She owned half this house. Hot tears of gratitude ran down her face for the only gift she'd ever had. And Bitty was selling it and had somehow managed to sign some papers in her name. It wasn't the fraud so much as being cheated of the knowledge of a birthright that made her ache. She'd never owned a thing; a tiny room in St Supplice, a few clothes, a small nest-egg. To her the reality of owning half a house was wrong, a great weight shackled with chains of greed around her aching ankles. Another wave of nausea passed. Bitty could have it, all of it. She'd leave again, run away from this awful place where everything was so important, so melodramatic. Every time anyone spoke it was a confrontation. Oh yes, the girls at Madame's had their little tantrums about missing stockings and the like, but it was all well within half an hour, at the most a day, a kiss, a gift and that was it. It didn't stain them. The thought of Bitty's large pink face loomed at her, the bitter turned-down mouth filling her with fear and disgust. She struggled off the bed to pack: Paris, anywhere, up into the sky free to float away like one of her smoke rings to anywhere but here. The bile rose in her throat and overcame her. She lurched again towards the bathroom. Once back on her bed she dozed, waking only for a moment to the sound of what she thought was breaking glass.

* * *

Titus waited for Bitty in the salon in the light of one small lamp. He heard the car return, the voice, her annoyance when she spotted the vultures through the kitchen window.

'What the hell? Titus! Titus!' He let her shout several times and then storm into the salon behind her advance guard of dogs, their toenails clattering on the polished wood.

'What the hell are those birds doing here? I thought I told you—'

'Sit down!' he ordered in a low voice. 'Sit down, shut up and listen. Then answer. If you can.' Bitty ignored him and headed for the drinks tray. Titus leaped across the room and intercepted her. He smashed the Gordon's to the floor.

'You must be mad.' She gaped at him.

'Norman Trail phoned.' He let it sink in. She turned an ugly red, guilt robbing her of a reply.

'Oh, what did he want?' By now she'd reached the fireplace and sunk into a chair.

'There is a chance that you can and will be prosecuted for forgery.' As he spoke she seemed to inflate with terror but no sound came from her open mouth. Titus patted the Peke to make her suffer.

'Poor thing, poor thing.' The only way to get the truth was to frighten her witless.

'I didn't mean it like that,' Bitty bleated.

'Mean it like what?' Titus kept his attention on the dog, fondling its ears the way Colombo would. Bitty's mind had stopped. There was no sound except the wind howling round the garden like an understudy for her tempests.

'Your allowance stops at the end of the week,' she pleaded eventually. 'What was I supposed to do? Desmond made me an offer on the house. I accepted.

There is no *money*. I did it for you, darling, really I did.' Titus stared at her with contempt.

'What papers is Minou supposed to have signed?'

'I did it for you, as I always have. It wasn't fair, why should she get half? Cody wouldn't have wanted her to have half if he'd lived. Who the hell is she? A half-caste, a nobody, a by-blow from a one night stand.'

'Like me?'

She faltered to a stop when she saw his face and gathered the dogs in case he hit her.

'I did it for you. Like today, the moment the dealer paid for the table, what did I do? I went straight out to get your birthday present.' The thought had never crossed her mind but what else could she say except, I want a drink. Oh, God how I want a drink. 'Your allowance stops at the end of the week.' Verbatim, the letter from Nolan's solicitor was running round and round in her head.

'You could get a job,' he suggested.

'Oh, don't be so stupid.' Even at this ghastly moment the idea was outrageous.

'Why not?'

'I've never had a job.' Bitty was forgetting her brief stint as an air hostess, since it didn't count. 'What on earth could I do?'

'Kennel maid for the vet in Gib?' Titus barked a laugh as Bitty rose to rush at him. He pushed her back into her chair.

'Why don't you just admit you're a greedy pig without a generous impulse in your fat soul. You were going to cheat Minou, of all people. Even now she tries to protect you.'

'What do you mean protect? What did she say to

Entrail?' Everything hinged on his answer. Oh, how she needed a drink!

'Nothing much. But she didn't give you away. I don't think she's interested. Disgusted but not interested.'

'You're quite sure she didn't say anything?' Bitty's colour started to come back as she remembered there was another Gordon's in the kitchen.

'Nothing.'

'Oh, she's a clever one.'

'Not clever.' The woman he'd walked round the town with saw things, heard things, understood things and all her life had happily made the best of whatever came her way. 'Proud, maybe; honest.'

Now she knew the fraud squad wouldn't be roaring up the drive at any moment, Bitty's fat knees wobbled with relief but she still wasn't going to risk standing. 'Proud? Don't tell me she couldn't do with a hundred and fifty grand.'

'So much?'

Bitty realised she'd said too much but waved it away. 'What does it matter how much, it wasn't morally hers, any of it. How many times do I have to tell you?'

'She owns half the house, correct?' One last time it had to be established without any doubt.

'It was all a mistake, a silly mistake. Why don't you tell her and we can come to some agreement and forget all about it.'

'You want *me* to tell her?'

'What does it matter who explains?' As long as it wasn't Entrail. What was there to worry about? Titus? Minou? 'She signs, Desmond completes and we're in the clear.'

Titus walked to the door putting space between them in case he did hit her.

'You never know . . .' Her plans came thick and fast, not least of which the sooner Titus left the sooner she could have a drink. 'If she's that proud she'll see what's fair and what isn't. She might not want the money. How do we know?'

'No,' Titus surprised her by agreeing. 'No, she might want to move in, not sell, live here. Then we can all be one happy little family.'

It hadn't crossed her mind. Aghast, Bitty sank off the chair and on to her knees in front of the unlit fire, gathering the dogs close again. Titus left to take some feverfew to Ingrid.

CHAPTER SEVEN

MINOU TRACED HER finger over the deep relief map on the travel agent's wall, over the wrinkled shadows of the Himalayas, down the crumpled spine of South America and the hot, yellow surface of Saudi Arabia, wearily considering anywhere that wasn't Andalusia. The Laccadives, she noticed, were in the Indian Ocean, some way north of the Maldives and not, as Jimmy had said, somewhere near Java. Hastings wasn't marked but Martinique was with a tiny bump for Mount Pele on latitude 13. Fragile and light-headed after the night of vomiting, Minou wished she could sit but all the seats were taken by a party of Japanese tourists having trouble with their reservations. A few gathered round the desk arguing with the Spanish girl in charge who glared at her computer screen, stabbing buttons with a scarlet fingernail. A two word message flashed, then vanished. One of the men eventually asked for the manual as the others awaited a further oracle from the blank screen. The man with the manual declared the fuse had gone. The Spanish girl clacked into the inner office for assistance but there was no one there. The Japanese broke into twittering dismay. The girl stalked out into the bright street and returned with a nine-year-old boy who, she informed them, was her brother. With much hand-waving and excitable entreaty she begged him to fix it. The child chewed gum and demanded a thousand pesetas, then vanished back into the street. The Japanese waited in a silent row. After a while the boy returned with a screwdriver and corkscrew. The Japanese nodded encouragement as the boy dismantled the plug with clumsy movements and put it back together. There was a bang, a shower of sparks and a considerable amount of smoke. The girl wailed, recovered herself, applied her lipstick, ordered everyone out of the agency and pulled down the blind.

The ferry was just pulling out of the harbour for Tangier. Why not Tangier? Too late. An opportunity missed, Minou stood in the hot sun wondering what to do next as the boat headed for the Straits. Each slow step drew her reluctantly back to the beach buggy and nearer to having to deal with Bitty. What would she say? What would she do? She looked with envy at vehicles parking and unparking, heading for the main square, up side roads and off to somewhere else. All those people who didn't have to go back to La Preciosa which should have been so perfect. Someone called her name.

Jimmy was sitting at one of the tapas bars. He looked almost smart, wearing a clean white shirt and a jaunty Panama hat. There was a pile of papers on the table. His companion was a golden-skinned young woman with a flow of hair, a twinkling ankle bracelet and a set of magnificent American teeth. Jimmy was pouring Champagne.

'Mornin', Minou.' He introduced her to Mrs Delahaye but didn't invite her to join them. 'Mrs Delahaye, that is Tracey, owns the *Dancing Lady*,' he explained with heavy significance. Mrs Delahaye shook hands with a whinnying laugh.

'How's Tom?' asked Minou.

'Windsurfing. He'll never learn. But we've got plans, we've got plans.' He poured more Champagne into Mrs Delahaye's glass. To her delight it frothed over the top.

'I must be going,' murmured Minou.

'Missing you already,' Mrs Delahaye called after her.

Bitty was slicing lemons in the kitchen. She stopped, knife poised at the sound of the beach buggy in the drive. She'd assumed Minou was still in bed. But she'd been somewhere. She was wearing jeans instead of that beach thing.

'Did you sleep well?' Ignore the unexpected, keep everything very normal. She sailed over and gave Minou an awkward kiss on the cheek and pulled a chair out for her at the kitchen table. 'It's too windy for breakfast out there.'

Minou glanced out of the window on to the terrace. How strange that the little birds could fly in such strong gusts without being blown away. 'I ate something that wasn't right.' All the words had gone, vanished, all those words she'd rehearsed, strong words she'd repeated to herself over and over again in the car. Madame would have been able to shut her up forever. What was it she used to say? '*Sortez!*' A scathing dismissal. But it was she who must *sortez* and the sooner the better. Wondering if her stomach was up to it she ventured the first cigarette of the day. Bitty poured some coffee for her in a big blue mug. There was no sign of Juanita.

'Milk? I forget if you take milk.' Bitty held the jug over the cup.

'Is the phone working?' Minou asked faintly. She could book a ticket by credit card to anywhere direct from the airport.

'Sugar?' It was like sweetness on a raw-nerved tooth. She breathed in and out a couple of times.

'I'm off, Bitty,' she said firmly and the sugar scattered on the tablecloth.

'Off?' Bitty had expected anger, tears or one of those sulks Minou used to go into. Even a tussle with litigation, but not this. There were still papers to be signed.

'Whatever do you mean, *off*?' Her pink face developed a silly smile. Minou blew a smoke ring at her and gave her a long look.

'Oh, you mean silly old Entrail and all that. You mustn't believe everything you hear.'

'I don't,' Minou replied, flinching from the plump hands about to grasp her own.

She stood up, dangling her car keys.

'It's all right, Bitty, you can have the house. I don't want it. It hasn't anything to do with me.' This was the deepest truth on the matter. She started towards the door.

'But you can't go!' cried Bitty, following her. 'You can't go yet. It's Titus's birthday. You can't go before his birthday, he'd be so disappointed. We're having a party,' she shrilled as Minou paused by the phone. Two more papers to sign, just two more. Bitty considered yanking the phone out of the wall. The dogs began to leap up and down, barking.

'You can't go yet.'

'It's better if I do.'

'But not before the birthday.' Bitty wheedled without shame standing in the doorway.

'It's all right, Bitty, I'm only going to the beach,' replied Minou and sidestepped her.

After three days and noisy nights the levante stopped in mid-gust. Without apology it just ceased to be. The only reminder were banks of sulking clouds and an oppressive heat pushing down on the *bojeo*. Beyond Tarifa the coastline was light and golden. But the weather was of little interest to Tom. Neither were the astounding variety of breasts on show at the topless and all-but bottomless beach. High, low, round, pointed, enticingly youthful, seductively mature, jiggling, swaying, shining with sun oil, all passed without a second glance. He was there to windsurf and the only thing that concerned him were the aching muscles of his body. The beginner's class, consisting of ten-year-old boys for the most part took place on an inland lagoon set back from the sea edge. His Norwegian instructor, not a day over seventeen, was kind and conscientious. Without comment or complaint he held Tom's collapsing body, pushed him back into a near-standing position and caught him again as he fell into the water. After two days of this hapless splashing in the shallows he was allowed to try surfing on the open sea. He suspected this was more for morale than progress. There, Tom discovered to his chagrin, most of the small boys had been promoted (after only a few hours' instruction) and were skimming if not with skill, certainly with enthusiasm. It took a long time to get the board, the mast and the sail correctly assembled. His wet suit, in which he thought he looked sinister and ridiculous, was very ill-fitting, full of sand and chafing his most tender parts. As he waded out into the water he felt as if he was being eliminated by a giant emery board. The Norwegian exhorted him to use stomach muscles he had long since forgotten. He floundered, wobbled, fell again then grimly pursued the board, which was bobbing off in the direction of North Africa. Legs like jelly, arms wrenching from their sockets, he had nothing left but will-power. With a final heave he got his feet into the right holds, hands on bar, leaned back and for a moment the wind was in the right place.

'Weight back! Relax!' called the Norwegian. For an astonishing twenty yards, Tom sailed precarious but triumphant. At which point six boards, red and blue, skimmed straight at him in an unbroken line. Inches away they split, three aside, flew past him and beached in a perfectly aligned row. Totally unnerved, Tom slithered into the sea and was immediately smothered by his yellow, plastic sail.

'The French champions,' the Norwegian told him. The champions stood on the beach looking at their feet as a grey-haired veteran gave them a blistering dressing-down, told them they were a load of shit and barked an order. They set off again: one, two, three, four, five, six, they skimmed, twisted, lifted, hit the water with a wet slap and tipped until almost horizontal. Within moments and at incredible speed they were far out to sea. The Norwegian chatted with the French instructor. Tom spat out some seawater. The Norwegian said something which he couldn't hear because his ears were blocked with sand. The Norwegian pointed at his multi-dialled watch. Tom was thankful to see him go. He heaved the board and all its bits up the beach and abandoned it just beyond the tide line. Without bothering to strip out of the awful wet suit he headed for Jimmy's car. Amanda was right about the mid-life crisis, he thought unhappily. Three days of that and he was an old man. Finished. All he wanted to do was lie down somewhere very quiet for a very long time.

The turning from the Cadiz road to Bolonia wasn't marked, but Ingrid had said he couldn't miss it because there was a building like a bunker with a blue door. The little road led through a valley of blond-tipped meadows beside a stream banked with oleanders. Praying that Jimmy's car wouldn't let him down but too weary to battle with its erratic gears, Tom drove between two great crags, so curiously angular they could have been man-made, until he got his first glimpse of the Atlantic and a long stretch of deserted beach. He coasted the last few yards and parked in the shade of a straw-roofed bar with wooden benches. He got out and untrapped his body from the wet suit, chucked it in the boot, and in his bathing suit, with a towel slung over his shoulder, walked slowly through the bent tamarisks and sand-dunes. In the distance he noticed three ancient looking pillars that didn't seem to have anything to do with anything else and remembered Ingrid's earnest information about a Roman ruin. Brown cows with wide-set horns wandered on the shore, ignoring him as he made his way on to the ripple-marked sand. At the far end of the beach two fishermen were mending nets beside a small wooden boat. A little girl with a red kite as large as herself tacked back and forth across the sand, entreating it to fly. As Tom strolled towards the boat he caught sight of a figure stretched out on a white towel. It was Minou, her arm thrown over her eyes, either asleep or in some distant place of her own. He paused, caught between his own need for solitude and being thought churlish if he ignored her. In such a wide and empty space it would be rude to ignore her. He was saved the decision when Minou sat up, as if some minute shifting of sand particles had warned her of his approach. She shaded her eyes with her hands. She wasn't naked, he noticed with relief. She was wearing the tablecloth she wore to the airport.

'Hullo. I hope I'm not disturbing you.'

'Not at all.' At a discreet ten feet away, Tom spread out his towel and lay down, conscious of the whiteness of his body. The sun was dazzlingly hot.

'It's much better over here. The other beach is horrible,' he told her, and for a few moments they discussed the virtues of the different beaches until he said, 'How are your ankles?' looking at her slim feet. There was only a slight blue mark.

A flock of birds flew overhead before she had time to answer. 'Juanita says that when the storks migrate over the Straits they do it in one long glide.'

'Juanita?' His habit of needed information was aroused.

'She works at Bitty's house. That's where I'm staying.'

The name Bitty rang a bell. 'Oh yes, Bitty. The lady with the dogs.' That blonde, booming woman for whom he'd smuggled in the dog pills.

'She's my sister.'

'Your sister?' He'd only seen Bitty for a moment when she dropped into Snitos and picked up the pills with scarcely a thank you. Puzzled, he was about to ask another question when Minou noticed his shoulders.

'Do you want some oil?' She tossed her bottle of Ambre Solaire on to his towel. He opened it and rubbed the stuff vigorously on to his chest and thighs.

'How long are you staying, or do you live here?'

'Not long.' Her brief answer cast a shadow on her

face. 'People who live here never come to the beach.' With no more explanation she rose and strolled to the water's edge and stood just out of reach of the neat rolls of breaking surf. Bending down she scooped water on to her face. The edge of the sarong, splashed with spray, clung to her slim legs. He thought how much more enticing, or was it just feminine, she looked than the sleek nakedness of the women on the other beach. As she rinsed her hands he let his guesses as to where she came from wander round the Latin countries of Europe. She walked back slowly and in one swift movement lay down on her towel, her legs and arms glistening with drops of water.

'You're a very neat beach person,' he commented, looking at the slim limbs without a grain of sand and her uncrumpled towel. 'We British don't seem to have the knack.'

'British beaches are very inhospitable.' She laughed and reached out for the oil.

'You know British beaches?'

'Hastings. It's grey. The only trouble with *this* beach is . . .' She stared out to sea as though searching. 'You can't see Jebel Moussa. I've got used to looking at it.'

'Are you the sort of person who wants to get to the top of a mountain, or just know what lies beyond it?' Again it crossed his mind that he must stop interrogating.

Minou didn't answer. She thought about what he'd said but didn't feel there was a time limit on her reply.

'Look at those cows.' She pointed to the large beasts plodding peacefully in single file along the edge of the dunes. 'They've been doing that forever.'

Tom took the remark as an evasion but Minou watched them until they were almost out of sight and he realised she meant what she said. She turned back to him and took up his questions.

'I'd like to go beyond the mountain. I don't particularly want to climb it, though. Couldn't one just fly over?'

'I don't know if that's allowed. But even if it is, what would you find. Shangri-La? Eternal youth?'

Again she took her time answering, rubbing oil on her legs with slow, gentle movements.

'If it were possible I'd like to find where I belong. I used to think family meant people. Maybe it means a place.'

'I hope you don't mind me asking, but where *do* you come from?'

She smiled. She'd had it put that way before. He wouldn't have apologised for his enquiry if she'd been white.

'Martinique, originally. My mother was Creole. She had a dress shop. Today they'd call it a boutique, I suppose.' She adjusted her sunglasses and closed her eyes.

They woke on their towelling islands at the same time. The little girl with the kite ran past backwards, her eye on the red shape in the sky. She gave a quick glance over her shoulder for their approval, stumbled and fell on the soft sand. The kite took a dangerous dive but she recovered her footing and jerked the string, her whole attention on the sky. When it was safely airborne again she gave them a coquettish little grin over her shoulder.

'Wishes are so simple at that age.'

'What would you wish for, now, then?' Another idiotic question. He'd never have risked that one with Amanda or the Carolines.

'Go back, get it right, start again, not different but the old life would be new.' Not sure what she meant, he interpreted it as Martinique.

'Perhaps,' she went on, 'I could go home and open up the dress shop.' It was so startlingly simple as a dream, Tom had to quell an impulse to kiss her. He jumped up.

'Time for a swim.'

She followed him to the water's edge and watched the waves just licking her toes. He dived in and out of waves for a while then came back looking younger and shaking himself like a dog. He was, she decided, a man of power. He had strong legs and a V-shaped furrow of wet fur on his chest. And she knew he had strong hands. But it wasn't just his physical appearance. Men of power, in her opinion, were the quiet ones. The ones who never raised their voices, *something* to do with concentration. Tom had concentration and a sense of himself. Unusual for a man to have a sense of himself when soaking wet. One of the fishermen called out to the little girl, who ran towards him. The kite whirled round and round, swooped and nose-dived into the sand.

'The day's on the wane.' Tom glanced at the sun as he rubbed himself down with his sandy towel. Minou picked up her basket. Barefoot, they walked through the dunes towards their cars. It reminded her of walking with Jean Luc. When they walked along the Seine, sometimes round the Louvre, they'd walk apart to see each other better. Sometimes they'd pretend they were strangers, tourists, gaping at treasures, warm in the knowledge that they could move in upon each other in their own, slow time. She pushed down the overwhelming sense of loss that rushed through her and walked on without breaking her pace. There was no sound except distant goat bells and a skylark.

'Do you think there's anything much to see?' Tom pointed to the three Roman arches. He couldn't remember what Ingrid had told him about them. 'Wonder what time it is?'

Minou said she didn't know but it must be getting on.

'I've got to get the car back. Jimmy wants me to meet some American woman. Hope he's not trying to set me up,' he added gloomily.

'Set you up?'

'A date or something. That's the last thing I need.'

Although she was of the opinion that was what he probably needed more than anything else, Minou said nothing and gave a little sigh, remembering for the first time that afternoon that he was English. 'Is it Mrs Delahaye?'

'Something like that.'

She decided to mind her own business. But as they strolled towards the Roman site Tom seemed in no great rush. They climbed over a boundary of sagging barbed wire. Among the long overgrown grass they could just make out the foundations of several small buildings grouped around a larger one. A few cobbled paths led in straight lines towards the beach and others towards the road. Here and there they caught the glint of a mosaic, ochre, blue and gold.

'How romantic.' Minou thought about fountains, roses and marble halls. 'I bet this was built by a Senator for a Moorish princess.'

'How's your Spanish?' called Tom. He'd found a plaque with sparse information. '*Pescado,* that's fish, isn't it?'

'Yes.'

'Sorry to disillusion you but it used to be a fish-salting depot. They caught the tuna on migration, salted 'em here and sent 'em back to Rome. Must have stunk to high heaven.'

She lit a cigarette and looked towards the two crags guarding the approach to the bay. They saw it all, the fishermen, the spikes, thick hands on nets, the drubbing and smashing of blood-stained water. But there were fountains too, she hoped, and chariots. Two storks whirred overhead and settled in gawky movements on the roof of a distant cottage.

'It's an amazing place this, isn't it?' she said.

'Yes,' he replied. 'But it makes you work for it.'

The cricket's agitation was erratic in the windless night and the bright moon hung high above a thick slug of mist over the Straits. Minou tried to read but still reasons and rationalisations flew around her head. Cody had given her his only gift and she was throwing it away. That she honestly didn't want this disturbing windfall didn't come into her reasoning. He'd remembered her, maybe he'd remembered Maman, but whatever his motives were didn't matter. Her own did. Scrupulously she examined each thought for her own truth and still her head ached with doubts. But it was her right, she kept telling herself, to do what she wanted and that was to run. Yet the thought of Titus loomed on her screen again and again. If anyone should own La Preciosa it was him, a birthright by virtue of blood. Bitty must have told him by now that Minou was leaving. She'd never be able to resist such a triumph. She switched off the light in an effort to blot out the picture of Titus's dark, reproachful eyes. The dogs were restless, barking at passing gnats, and distant ships lamented like sad cows. She switched the light on again. The paperback was old, the pages brown at the edges, sections coming away from the spine. A trickle of sand spread across her pillow. A mosquito tracked towards her and a mad moth flapped against the light bulb. Suddenly the curtains blew, whooshed up to the ceiling like startled wraiths, a little wind whirled round the room as if a giant door in the heavens had opened to create a draught. Just as abruptly it stopped. She almost heard it laugh. The book fell to the floor. Brushing the sand from the pillow, then turning out the light, Minou resigned herself to another sleepless night. She thumped the pillow and fell into an uneasy dream. Bitty, swollen into a giant ball about to roll across the room, smashing everything in her path and flattening Minou to a paste. She woke with a start. There was someone in the room. It was Titus, standing at the foot of her bed, outlined against the moonlight.

'It's me,' he said in a funny, cracked voice. She leaned over to switch on the light, holding the sheet against her naked body.

'Don't put the light on.'

'Why not?' She caught the smell of his aftershave. 'What's the matter?' He was wearing nothing but a small towel round his waist.

'Nothing. Can I have a cigarette?' They both reached for the Gitane on the bedside table. His arm bumped against hers. He slid his hand down to her wrist and handcuffed it between his finger and thumb. Her heart sank. He'd come to plead, to demand, that she would stand with him against Bitty. For a moment he was still and then his body lurched at her with rushed awkwardness and to her astonishment and then dismay she realised that he was making some sort of anguished pass at her. His weight across the sheet pinned her down. In the half light she could see his eyes rolling like a nervous horse about to bolt, which she realised was nerves rather than insanity, and stiffened in an attempt to hold back a shrieking giggle rather than offend. For a moment she was back again in the locker room at Hastings High, the smell of sour socks, knickers and rude, ugly giggles. Those days of girls untaught in the beauty of themselves, whose sexual education was only covert readings of rude bits in the Bible. But whatever happened this was no moment to deride.

'Titus, what on earth are you *doing*?' Snaking out from under him she slipped off the bed and knotted herself into the sarong. He thrust his face down into her pillow.

'Titus?' She shook his brown shoulder. 'What's going on?' He didn't reply. She lit a cigarette and perched on the end of the bed waiting. Eventually, for lack of air, he turned his head.

'Thought that's what you wanted.' The words came from behind clenched teeth. She tried to remember if at any time she'd led him on.

'No, Titus, we're friends, you and I.' He looked at her as if he doubted it. 'I mean, you're a very attractive young man, you must know that, but it doesn't mean . . .'

'Thought that's what you wanted,' he repeated sulkily. 'It's what everyone else seems to want.'

'Well, I don't and apart from what I want, I'm far too old for you.'

'Didn't think you'd let that sort of thing bother you.'

'It doesn't,' she replied, adjusting herself to the idea that it did. Not bother exactly, but an innate sense of what was appropriate stood four square between them like a stern adjudicator. Titus inhaled deeply. In the faint light he looked so healthy and seemed a little chirpier. Relieved, probably. Her withdrawal from his nearness and the smell of his body suddenly rose like a tidal wave above her head, about to crash down. She raised her arm as if to ward it off, saw the intentness of his gaze and turned it into a stretch.

'Jesus, it's hot. It's because of the house, isn't it?'

A bulls-eye. He nodded.

'Titus, do you mean to say you thought that by sleeping with me you'd save the house?' Although at a loss to understand his reasoning she knew she was right.

'Sort of. Sort of last ditch.'

'Thank you.' His seduction manners left a lot to be desired, she thought, even in one so young. But that wasn't the issue. She didn't know whether to laugh or be very angry.

'Titus, you do realise what that makes you, don't you? To say nothing of what it would make me.' Such a strong moral line surprised him.

'Sort of.'

'There's no *sort of* about it and you know perfectly well what I'm talking about.' He was now trembling and since it wasn't with desire she took it to be delayed shock.

'Don't you have a girlfriend?'

'Oh, I did once,' he assured her. 'Got drunk at the disco. There was this German girl. She seemed keen, relentless really, so I thought I'd give it a try. Had to sometime. It was a disaster,' he admitted in a low voice followed by a snort of unhappy laughter. 'I suppose it always will be after . . .' He paused on the verge of some monstrous admission. Minou looked up at the white ceiling, waiting, but he clammed up again and put his face back in her pillow.

'Oh, Titus, sit up.' Reluctantly he obeyed. 'Now,' she ordered, taking his hand and placing it on the inside of her wrist, 'feel my pulse.' Gingerly he laid his fingers on her vein.

'Got it?'

'Think so.'

'Good.' She lifted his hand and placed it where she hoped her heart was and ignored his look of panic. 'Can you feel it, my heart?'

After a moment he said he thought he could.

'Good.' She gave him back his hand. 'That's all there is to it. Just another human being, another life, someone as real as you are. When you make love just remember that and everything will be all right. The rest is mindless, heartless and what most men want. Of course it's all they get and they wonder why it's not enough. They forget there is someone else there too. It's sad.'

'Oh, it's all too complicated for me. I don't want to have anything to do with it. One doesn't *have* to, does one?'

'I suppose not,' was all she could reply to such a novel idea. The nape of her neck was soaking and they both shone with a thin film of sweat as if they'd been locked in a steamy embrace for a long time.

'If we had a pool we could swim.' It was a good idea. It would calm the surge of longing that he'd roused in her.

'We could go to the beach, go for a drive.' She went out on to the balcony, stepping carefully over a mess of grey droppings. The five swallow chicks were crushed into their nest, their tails drooping down. She came back rubbing the stiffness of her dry bikini between her hands. There was a great part of this story missing and now she'd started she was determined to get to the sad heart of what went wrong.

They drove in silence. With his black Spanish hat tipped over his eyes, Titus was giving quite a passable impression of Clint Eastwood having a wary doze. He'd dressed in black boots, black trousers and a black shirt with silver buttons. She thought it strangely formal for a night drive but it probably made him feel secure. As they passed Tarifa the beach-side bars and little shops were still open. The proprietors and their tired wives sat in quietness in the doorways after their last customers had gone to squander more of the hot night. Minou drove until they reached the disco car-park and stopped beside a row of windsurfers' caravans. All their doors and windows were open. People strolled along the beach as if it were still day, eating, drinking and playing music beside scattered bonfires. A young German twanged a bolero on his guitar and was shouted down by a Teutonic 'Home on the Range'.

'Do you want a drink?' Titus leaned against the beach buggy, staring at the moon. Minou went to buy the drinks. He had two Scotches and a couple of sherries. She drank a vodka, then another, and neither of them spoke as disco music blared across the car-park, contaminating the black sky and the stars. Titus looked away as a naked couple chased each other up and down the moonlit sand-dunes.

'Tell me, Titus.' There was an endless, gummed-up silence. She went to pay for the drinks, bought a bottle of Champagne and got the barman to open it for her. He was still staring at the moon, his face wet with tears when she got back. She handed him the Champagne.

His lips closed round it like a calf, as he took three urgent gulps.

'I suppose it started at school,' he muttered. Minou caught her breath and could have kicked herself for not having thought of it before. Of course, he'd been to an English Public School. She'd heard stories about them. Once or twice Englishmen had found their way to Madame's. The girls had shaken their heads in disbelief. To her, homosexuality was understandable. Just. And then only when she didn't think about it too much. One or two of the girls at Madame's had professed to prefer women but she'd never been able to take that too seriously either. Such a waste of time and should the subject ever arrive it was dismissed with this light judgement. But deep down she thought it blasphemous.

'What happened? You must tell me.' His white face glittered.

'I was so *pretty*.' He spat the word out.

'And you were assaulted? Seduced? Is that why you didn't want to go back to school?' He took her question seriously.

'Assaulted? I suppose so, but no more than a bit of groping. It happened to most of the younger boys. Seduced? Never!' She felt relief, then a swift curiosity.

'Why did you hate it?'

'If you look like me, life is hell.' It was as if his beauty was a hideous deformity. 'When the dog bit me, when I still had on the bandages, even over my eyes, I made a sort of blind date with myself and I prayed I'd be hideous. But I wasn't.'

'Then?' He turned and looked at her.

'It was *her*. She didn't care. In a way I think she wanted me to be ugly. I tried to tell her . . . I tried so hard to tell her, what hell it was at school: a pretty boy with some sort of dago father, but Nolan was paying and I was out of her way. She never listened to me.' Minou watched him, sorrow fighting the rage in her stomach. The strobe lights from the disco flashed and passed, leaving them in darkness. Her blood began to rise in a terrible way, as if a violent poison was coursing through her.

'She is so *pink*. She makes me feel so impotent!' The word was like a death cry.

'Oh, *merde*!' She hurled the empty Champagne bottle into the dunes. 'Let's get out of here.' Minou didn't know what she was going to do, how to heal the scars left by Bitty's mindlessness, but it was her duty to do something. A woman's duty was to make a man a man.

'You'd better put your shoes on,' he commented, looking at her bare feet. 'There might be broken glass.' He turned to get into the passenger seat.

'No!' she commanded in a voice she didn't feel to be her own. She pointed at the steering wheel. 'Here! You drive,' she said and tossed him the keys.

The stars flew past and the great fields roamed by the black bulls fell away on either side.

'A, B, C,' she instructed. 'Accelerator, brake, clutch. Flick that thing there, it means you're going to overtake.'

Titus negotiated his way past a truck, changing down instinctively and then accelerating. As they sped past the bunker with the blue door, the turning to Bolonia, she thought about asking him to turn, but didn't. That afternoon with Tom had been so good. It could be all right with Tom. It could even be wonderful. Then she remembered she was drunk and brought her attention back to Titus and the road ahead. It was clear. His hands relaxed on the wheel and by the time they reached Chiclana he could drive. He danced the car across the road, overtook with surety and dimmed for oncoming cars with well-timed courtesy.

'Let her go!'

His hat blew off. He started singing 'Guantanamera'. 'Almost as good as flying!' he shouted. Minou gave a satisfied little smile as they drove on to Seville to watch the sunrise.

CHAPTER EIGHT

The telephone was on good form, no buzzing, no deadpan sulks and it only took dialling three times to get through to that idiot Entrail.

'Good-morning Mr Trail.' Bitty used her sunniest voice and why shouldn't she? Minou had capitulated without a murmur. She rotated her ankle and assured him Mona's idiotic mistake could have happened to anyone. Mr Trail used his most apologetic voice back.

'My dear Mrs Nolan, what can I say?' he ended at last, having said it all over again several times and adding that Sir Desmond had been most understanding about the delay. 'Normally I'd be only too delighted to drive over myself with the papers but alas . . .'

Her ankle was definitely slimmer. She decided to let him meander on. It was only when he suggested posting the damned things that she snapped back into action.

'For God's sake, don't do that! It'll take weeks. Look, Miss Latour is very much better so we'll come to see you.' Entrail started mouthing gallant protests but Bitty cut him short. 'Of course it will be tiring for her and we mustn't risk a relapse but if you have the papers ready and waiting, say in reception, she'll sign and be off in a flash.' That way, with luck, she could get Minou in and out of the office without Entrail setting eyes on her. You never knew, the woman was quite capable of batting her eyelashes and asking stupid questions. Entrail, alerted to the dangers of a seriously sick woman on his premises, agreed to an appointment that afternoon. Singing, Bitty went to weigh herself.

'I've only lost a pound, there must be something wrong with those scales.' The kettle boiled. Reluctantly Bitty sliced another lemon, put it in a glass and poured the boiling water over it.

'Like some tea?' This was for Minou's benefit. She'd entered the kitchen silently and was on her way to the garden. She didn't answer, angrily certain that if she spoke the only thing that would escape her mouth would be a low and very savage snarl.

'Our appointment is at three. Is that all right with you?' Bitty eyed her over the rim of the steaming glass.

'Certainly,' agreed Minou coldly, passing through the kitchen with light steps. A distant look and on into the garden without even commenting on the weather, which Bitty considered a bit offish.

'Oh well, suit yourself.' Remembering she hadn't spoken to Annie for a day or so she settled down to make good use of the phone while it was in an obliging mood. With a face set in gloom, Juanita swept round her and the dogs. The Feria was about to start; her granddaughter's dress was a triumph, she'd been paid; but there was something in the air she didn't like.

For lack of anything better to do, Minou settled herself on the edge of the fountain and started work on her nails. Normally they were round and short, but she noticed, with grim satisfaction, that since she'd stopped sewing they were quite long. Rather tigerish. Fishing through her manicure bag, she settled for scarlet. Working the emery board back and forth in a gentle rhythm she stared at Jebel Moussa, so solid and magnificent. She breathed in and out but it didn't work, unaccustomed anger filling her with a desire to scream or shout. Titus, twenty-one tomorrow, with no more of a future than to be crushed by Bitty into a life of hate, rage biting him away in chunks. Bitty's social voice rang loud on the warm breeze from the kitchen.

'We're having a little do for Titus, his twenty-first. Yes, how time flies. No, my dear, not here. It's the Feria so the staff are off and anyway, the table's gone. Jimmy's? Yes, it's fun, slumming it with the young . . .' Juanita stopped banging into furniture with the broom and was making a great to-do of shaking mats on the terrace. The Peke sneezed and flopped down the steps and settled at Minou's feet, looking at her as if it were all her fault. It was followed by Bitty waving her notepad.

'We're having it at Jimmy's.' She plonked herself down next to Minou, who concentrated on lacquering the nail of her little finger. The colour was called Desire. Bitty stared with distaste, the word slut popping into her mind.

'That'll be nice, won't it? Jimmy's perfectly capable of turning out a decent meal if he puts his mind to it.' There was no response from Minou, now on the third finger of her left hand.

'The party. I'm talking about the party.' Fed up with Minou's sulk, she could have shaken her. After all it was her idea to have a party. 'It was your idea,' she reminded her.

'Was it?' Minou couldn't remember but didn't think it was. Bitty skimmed down the list.

'There's Annie and her husband, that's if he comes which he probably won't, which doesn't matter because he's such an old bore; those Americans might come; Jimmy – I suppose we'd better ask him because he'd come anyway; that brother of his; Ingrid; Titus; me and you. That makes?'

'Ten.' Minou screwed the top on the varnish bottle without smudging her nails.

'If Annie's husband doesn't come we'll be a man short. I wonder?' Bitty stared innocently at a passing swallow. 'I wonder if I should invite Desmond?' There were several good reasons why she should. If Minou suddenly did a bunk or backed out at the last minute, Desmond would be more than persuasive. Also, she thought happily, she'd lost at least five pounds no matter what those stupid scales said.

'You know Desmond, don't you? Desmond Macmahon? No, no, you probably wouldn't.' She was right, the name meant nothing to Minou.

'Such a charming man. It would be a nice gesture.'

'What time is it?' Minou stood up abruptly.

'Time we were off.' Bitty battled with the impulse to handcuff Minou to her wrist as they walked back to the house.

'You've got your passport, haven't you?' Minou nodded, stopped, turned and took one last look at Jebel Moussa. Bitty, who thought she was praying for some idiotic reason, went round the side of the house to the Range Rover, followed by the dogs.

The battery was flat, not even one little cough of life. Panic seized her by the throat as she felt the gods begin to turn. Minou joined her in the drive, her face thin and wearing dark glasses.

'Damn and blast!' Sweat poured as Bitty gave the key another hopeless turn. With a heaving gesture of despair she gave up.

'We'll have to take that thing of yours.' They both turned to the beach buggy. There were tyre marks on the gravel, a patch of oil and a great space where it should have been.

'It's gone!'

'It's been stolen!' cried Bitty, whose mind worked faster than Minou's. Minou was about to say that it had been there earlier, when she and Titus had crept giggling into the house, drunk and happy. Antonio pushed the squeaking wheelbarrow past them.

'*Donde está la coche de la Señora*?' shouted Bitty.

Without turning his head he replied, '*Titus ha partido con dos gallinazos.*'

'Don't be ridiculous.' Bitty ran round the side of the house and scanned the lawn but there was no sign of the vultures.

'*Los gallinazos* are gone! But he can't have— He can't drive!'

'He can now.' Antonio chuckled for the first time in twenty years. The phone jangled from the kitchen. The dogs all started barking.

'Oh, shut up and let me think!' Juanita slouched out of the house to tell Bitty the phone was ringing.

'Well, answer it, woman!' Antonio, halfway down the drive, shouted over his shoulder to Juanita that Titus had taken the car. Juanita crossed herself, burst into tears and wrung her hands, beseeching mercy from a flock of storks flying overhead. The phone rang on. Bitty hurled herself into the house, remembering the dealer from Jerez had said he'd call if he found a buyer for the sideboard.

'We'll have to take Jimmy's car. Go and tell him!' she yelled back at Minou. Sucked in by her tremendous will, Minou started back across the lawn, taking the short-cut to El Snitos that Titus had taken a few nights before.

Tom woke at midday in his tiny room behind Jimmy's kitchen. The sun streamed into his eyes, the heat was outrageous and a sense of doom clogged his heart as he tried to raise his sticky body from the sheet and fell back. His throat was parched and his vision, if not exactly double, was seriously blurred. Right again, Amanda, time to get glasses. As he lay there the sound of bracelets jangling for joy struggled through the thick fog of the night before. It had been a long, long night. Jimmy sang sea shanties for most of it. Mrs Tracey Delahaye filtered back, she of the bracelets. A nice girl despite her ridiculous name and a tendency to shriek 'Let's live!' every so often. With a thundering shock he remembered. He'd signed a cheque! Amid the din of the Feria parade, whirling streamers, harsh guitars and showers of rose petals, he'd signed a cheque! He could see it now, his hard-earned, neatly-organised future reduced to noughts on a bit of paper sliding away into Tracey Delahaye's Hermès wallet.

'Whoops!' She fished a streamer out of his drink and told him she had an account at the National Arab Bank in Knightsbridge.

'Dontcha just lurve Harvey Nichols?' And Jimmy said it over and over again.

'It's got a Lloyd's A certificate and you don't come by that easily.' But it was all too easy to come by a yacht. All you had to do was sign and shake hands a lot.

'Rise and shine!' Jimmy, brutally cheerful, stood over his bed with a briefcase and a lager.

'I say, old chap, do us a favour.' Tom waved the lager away.

'Another?' The nerve of the man left him numb.

'Nothing much, Coca-Cola man. Sort him out, would you?'

'You mean pay him.' Tom flung himself down flat. 'No. You pay him.'

'Gotta dash, things to see to in Gib.'

'What things?'

'Things. Things. Insurance and things.'

'Leave a cheque and I'll give it to him.' Jimmy shook his head.

'Problem there.'

'What?' snapped Tom in a voice that would have made Margaret Thatcher quake.

'Goat ate it.' Jimmy breezed off, whistling 'A Life On the Ocean Wave'.

Tom quelled the impulse either to bellow or weep, deciding the only manly thing to do was have a decent breakfast.

'Is there any marmalade?' he asked Ingrid and wished he hadn't. Rock still, chalk white, she was sitting on a barstool with a wet cloth over her eyes. One of the Carolines had suffered from migraine and he knew the signs.

'Why don't you go back to bed?' An attempt to shake her head failed. He thought of offering her a cup of coffee but decided it would be cruel to force decisions on her. He put down his cup with care and tried to eat his toast silently. The sun filtered through the bamboo lattice to the sound of gentle snores of the overdraft-eating goat. *The Independent* was days out of date. Turning for solace to Trollope, he found to his dismay that that too had turned stale. Things were very low when you couldn't rely on Trollope. Staring out at the haze over the Straits, he thought gloomily about yachts.

'Anyone at home?' Minou paused in the doorway, one foot lightly touching the ground as if she were about to speed off again. Ingrid waved a limp hand.

'Good-morning.' Tom rose, not bothering to correct himself even though it was well past two. 'He's in Gib.'

'*Merde!*' Her hand made a small, anxious fist. 'We needed his car. That is, Bitty does. It's urgent.' Despite the supposed urgency, Tom detected a little gleam of relief in her eyes.

'What'll it be?' He went behind the bar. To his surprise he felt rather jolly there.

'A Coke,' she replied absently.

'Sorry, we're out. How about a Fanta?'

'No, thank you. When will Jimmy be back?'

Ingrid shook her head and gave a little yelp.

'Ingrid, please go back to bed. I can manage. It's not as if there'll be a rush.' Tom opened the fridge door and deliberated between three sorts of horrible Spanish Champagne. For a moment Minou thought how like his brother he was.

'Hopeless, but all is not lost.' He located the orange juice.

'Hopeless,' muttered Ingrid and winced as the cork popped.

'Buck's Fizz?' Tom suggested.

'That's so English.' He wondered why Minou laughed but was glad she did.

'Cheers! Might as well celebrate. It's not everyday one buys a yacht.' Minou hopped up on to the barstool next to Ingrid and gave a clap of excitement.

'You did it, then! Oh bravo, bravo!'

'God knows what we're going to do with it.' After all, what did one do with a yacht except sail around? Or perhaps live in it? She interrupted his thoughts with a little grin.

'Depends whether you're the sort of person who just looks at the sea or wonders what's on the other side.'

'Aunts,' whimpered Ingrid suddenly from behind the cloth. 'Aunts, that's all we are, aunts crawling around the earth.' They looked at each other and guessed she must mean ants, which wasn't much better.

'Ingrid.' This time it was an order. 'Go and lie down.'

The damp cloth still over her eyes, Ingrid slipped off her stool, swayed for a moment and wobbled out of the bar towards her mobile home. They heard the door slam and winced for her. A silence fell between them.

'Will Jimmy be long?'

'I don't know. But probably, yes.' He was on the verge of asking her out to lunch when she sighed and explained again that Bitty had this important appointment in Gib.

'I'm supposed to go too,' she said flatly. Any temptation to get the whole story out of her in thirty seconds flat was pushed away by the arrival of the Coca-Cola man.

The Coca-Cola man was dark and melancholy and had a cleft palate. The only recognisable word in his woeful Andalusian stream of grievance was peseta, which he said quite often. Tom went through the shaming list of receipts for deliveries on credit (which went back to the previous November) cursing Jimmy. He offered the dejected man a beer and after a long discussion he convinced him that although he was Jimmy's brother he was a man of honour. Furthermore he was willing, if not eager, to pay the debt with a Eurocheque. The Coca-Cola man brightened a bit at the word Eurocheque and they settled down to work out the exchange rate. Minou, assisting with the language problem, didn't help matters by having to translate it all into francs first. It took an hour. Vindicated, the Coca-Cola man departed, leaving six crates and Tom two hundred pounds down. By the time he'd humped the crates into the store room he was sweating from the sheer madness of it all.

'I need another drink.'

'What the hell do you think you're doing?' Bitty stood in the doorway blocking out the sun. 'Don't you realise what time it is?' She shook the small watch on her fat wrist under Minou's nose as she took in the Champagne and the espadrille dangling from her slim, brown foot. Need she ask more? Anything in pants! Slut!

'Would you like a drink?'

Bitty ignored Tom's polite offer and drained Minou's glass. 'Even if we take a taxi it'll be too late. Really, this is too much.'

'But Jimmy's already in Gib; he'd left when I got here. There was nothing I could do,' protested Minou.

'You could have come back and told me.' Excluded by the blankness of their expressions Bitty turned on her heel and noticed Ingrid's Beetle.

'We'll take that!' She started up the drive in a fury.

'Bitty, please! Don't wake Ingrid, she's not well.'

'I'm not going to wake her, I'm going to borrow her damn car.' Bitty's voice turned into a wail as she emerged backside first from the little car, hair spilling over her face and stupid eyes brimming with tears of rage.

'The keys! Where are the keys?' She banged on the door of the mobile home with her fist.

'Oh Bitty, please don't. She's so ill.'

'What do you mean ill? She's not here!' The door burst open. Bitty turned from the empty caravan, defeated.

'Don't think I don't know what's going on.' Her voice was heavy with malice. 'And while we're at it, where the hell is Titus?'

After the stretch of road between Algeciras and the *bojeo* came a series of curves before El Snitos. Titus rounded the last bend in time to see Bitty, heading through the gates, on foot and in a state. He slowed down and came to a halt on the main road. The feverfew for Ingrid in his pocket, he walked silently to the caravan. He'd come back later and show her how to boil it up. Bitty was giving someone in the bar hell, very loudly. The skinny grey horse in the nearby field stopped shaking flies from its head and listened sadly. Titus knocked on the door of the caravan twice and opened it. Inside it was suffocating, the branches of overhanging eucalyptus tapping on the metal roof and Ingrid, wrapped in a patchwork quilt, lay flat as a plank on her bunk.

'You need some fresh air,' he said unsympathetically.

'I can't,' she moaned, art deco patterns swirling in ugly zigzags behind her eyes.

'Yes, you can. Yes, you can.' Today anyone could do anything. For a start the vet in Algeciras had been more than obliging in putting down the vultures. One look in the carton and he'd agreed there were more than enough vultures in the world, a glut, so to speak, from which Titus gathered he must have troubles of his own. Joyfully he parted with forty thousand pesetas (borrowed from Antonio), which left enough to treat himself to a drink at the Reina Christina. In the cool marble bar he sipped thoughtfully on a daiquiri with a faraway, brooding expression as he weighed up the choice of telling Bitty about the vultures or keeping the power of a secret. Rant and rave as she may, they were gone and there wasn't a damn thing she could do about it.

'Jesus, these Spanish guys are something else. Did you ever see eyes like that?' Two attractive American women in expensive, minimal bikinis gazed at him from their table by the pool. He pretended not to hear their remarks. Not remarks so much as eulogies.

'I wasn't looking at his eyes,' sighed the other without bothering to lower her voice. He finished his drink without haste, feeling kindly towards them. Driving back, he waved graciously to all those on the roadside.

'It really is too inconsiderate . . .' Bitty's voice found them in the caravan. Ingrid covered her head and moaned.

'Oh, come on, Ingrid.' Titus pulled her to a sitting position, unwrapped her from the patchwork quilt and stood her up, noticing for the first time what nice, long, white legs and elegant feet she had.

'My glasses; my glasses.' He grabbed her granny specs from a shelf of books in Swedish, English, Spanish and, of all things, Latin.

'No, no. The dark ones.' She managed to reach for her dark glasses by the bedside. 'Where are we going?'

'Shh . . .' He half carried her out to the road, pushed her into the beach buggy and sped off in the direction of Jerez. Oh, what a wonderful day! He'd outwitted Bitty again. In total trust, Ingrid sat hunched behind the dark glasses until they bumped over the mountain track originally designated for the vultures' release.

'Feeling better?'

'A bit,' she replied with surprise.

'Works really fast, that feverfew. Lucky I remembered.' She was about to remind him that he hadn't given it to her, but it seemed a shame to spoil it for him. He realised she didn't know a joke when she heard one. But that too was funny. As he laughed out loud he wondered if at last this was what it meant like to feel young.

The midges began to swarm and the sun began to set when Jimmy's car creaked to a standstill outside the bar, the back seat piled with nylon rope and plastic buckets. He got out, clutching a pile of marine charts.

'Evenin', Minou.' He helped himself to a glass of cheap Spanish Champagne, smacked his lips, shook his head and poured another.

'My God, that stuff's vile. Well, we've done it, we're off.' Minou felt a pang of longing to be off too. Away from Bitty, away from Spain, away, away, away.

'Where?' asked Tom.

'The Laccadive, man, the Laccadive.'

'Might help if we knew where it was.'

Jimmy brushed this aside. 'Don't be like that. It's over there,' which indicated that it was somewhere behind the pump house.

'Want a bet?' Tom felt he had to challenge at some point.

'Name it!' Jimmy flipped open his wallet, then remembered there was nothing in it. 'Tell you what, everyone guesses where it is, writes it down and the one who's nearest gets to choose where we go.' Tom and Minou gaped at him. 'Now, what could be fairer than that?'

'OK, you're on.' The two men shook hands.

'You see,' Jimmy told Minou, 'if you can't dazzle them with brilliance, baffle them with bullshit.'

'There is just one thing,' Tom reminded him. 'If none of us knows where it is, how are we going to find out?' He leaned back and crossed his arms over his chest. Jimmy gave this line of logic some thought and decided they needed an atlas. Minou, about to tell them there was a large relief map in the travel agent's, was forestalled.

'Anyone got an atlas?' No one had.

'The travel agents—' she began.

'Ingrid will have one. Where is Ingrid?' Jimmy looked around.

'Vanished,' Minou explained. 'She had a migraine and vanished.'

'Migraine, euphemism for sex starvation. The trouble with Ingrid is her love life. Clever, though, I'll give her that. Clever.' The three of them looked towards the mobile home where Ingrid was supposed to be suffering but wasn't.

'She must have an atlas, she's the type. She wouldn't mind if we looked.' Jimmy started up the drive.

'Just a minute.' Tom caught up with him in two strides. 'We'll both go . . .'

They returned, each holding a corner of a dog-eared school atlas.

'Told you so.' They all looked at it.

'Now what?'

'First, another round.' Jimmy filled the glasses. 'Then each person writes where it is on a bit of paper.' He rummaged around and found the bill pad behind a carton of crisps and tore off three pieces of paper.

'What if it's not in the atlas?'

'It will be.' Jimmy scribbled Java on his bit of paper and handed the pencil over to Minou.

'But . . .' She flushed and looked away. The shock of being included took her breath away, as if someone had heard her silent longing to run.

'Go on, make a guess,' Jimmy urged. Then, noticing her reticence, added, 'Can't go without you, you're our mascot.' She looked at Tom, to see how he was taking this idea, waiting for his affirmation. He looked back steadily in a way that told her she had to make her own decision. She hesitated for a moment then scribbled on the paper fast, as if the adventure might disappear unless she made it real with words. She handed the pencil to Tom, who wrote down Honduras for want of any other ideas.

'Now what? Shouldn't we put them in a hat or something?' The three slips of paper sat on the mahogany bar.

'It's a bet, not a lucky dip.' Jimmy leafed through the atlas slowly, stopping on the places he'd been to.

'Oh, come on.' Tom grabbed it from him and turned to the index.

'The Laccadive, Indian Ocean.' Jimmy unfolded Minou's paper and placed it between Honduras and Java. 'OK, Minou, you win. Where's it to be?'

She took a deep breath. 'Martinique,' she said in a little voice that was almost a question.

They took it well. Tom was, if anything, filled with relief that they wouldn't be going anywhere near the China Seas with Jimmy at the helm.

'Why not?' Jimmy, unconcerned where they went, unrolled a map of the Atlantic and spread it out on the table. 'Where is it?'

'There!' cried Minou, pointing as if they'd just sighted land.

'There's a lot of sea,' Tom commented cautiously as neither of the others seemed to have noticed.

'Yes, but it's quite straight. Look.' She measured the distance with the straw from her drink. 'Look, quite straight, no bends, no corners anywhere.' He remembered dark things about women on ships. Then remembered the silk-covered state room, Tracey Delahaye's king-sized bed and had a clear, clear picture of Minou, dark, naked, laughing on the white satin. Jimmy rolled up the map and began to talk about trade winds in a matter-of-fact way. Minou slipped on her espadrilles.

'By the way,' she remembered, 'did Bitty or anyone mention the party?'

'What party? Who's party?'

'Titus, it's his twenty-first tomorrow.'

Jimmy beamed. 'Sea-bass – we'll have sea-bass. Used to do it in China.'

'Do you bake it in salt?' she asked.

'Of course,' replied Jimmy, who hadn't any idea. 'Sea-bass. What about lobster?' As they discussed the menu Tom stared back at the sea, thinking what a lot of it there was between him and Martinique.

'It would be nice to have—' Minou broke off suddenly, fearing to intrude on Bitty's territory as a hostess. 'You'd better talk to Bitty about it. But I'm glad it's you who's doing the party for Titus. It's good for him to feel someone cares.'

'We all do, always have, but he doesn't want to notice,' Jimmy replied with a perception that startled her. She darted forward and kissed him on the cheek, which Tom thought unnecessary.

'Do you want a lift?' he asked as Minou prepared to leave.

'It's all right, I'll walk, take the short-cut.' However, he found himself walking beside her until they reached the road.

'I knew where the Laccadives were,' she admitted as they waited for a lorry to pass.

'I know.'

'No, what I mean is, I *really* knew, before.' It sounded as if she were confessing to being a cheat.

'But that's the whole point,' Tom said reasonably. 'Gambling isn't guessing, it's knowing.'

'That was all right, wasn't it?' Titus thought he'd better ask as Ingrid appeared to have been in a trance for the past twenty minutes. She stretched her naked, white limbs, rapidly turning pink, on a stretch of rough grass high in the Sierra Cabrito.

'It cures migraine.' It was difficult for her to talk, overwhelmed with a new conviction that there must be a God because He'd let it happen for the first time with Titus. After that everything was hazy.

'I thought it was good.' Actually he thought it was magnificent, he was magnificent. Whatever overtook him, possessed him, guided him to do the most unthought-of things, was magnificent. He'd tried to keep in mind what Minou had said about there being another person there, another beating heart, but for a moment he was hardly there himself. The only trouble was it didn't last long.

'Yes, I thought it was good, too,' Ingrid said thoughtfully, which was enough for both of them. Titus rose and zipped up his jeans. After a while she added, 'Anyway, we don't have to do it a lot, do we?'

'Not if we don't want to,' said Titus, who already wanted to again.

'Just once in a while and then only when we want to.' Ingrid got to her feet, pulled on her T-shirt and brushed bits of wild thyme out of her hair. She had the imprint of a fern on her bottom. Titus laughed.

'What's funny?'

'Oh, nothing. I'm going to buy you a hat.' She'd look good in a hat. One of those ones with a large brim that dipped and curved. He took her hand and guided her down the rocks, thinking about what a nice girl she was.

'I shouldn't tell Minou, though,' he advised when they reached the beach buggy. 'She sets a lot of store by passion and all that stuff.'

'Don't worry.' Ingrid put on her dark glasses and lit a cigarette. 'I'll try my contact lenses again, it gives a sort of starry look.'

He thought she looked pretty starry already. He let out the clutch.

'Not that it's anybody else's business.'

CHAPTER NINE

A PERFECT MOON was on the rise over Ceuta and the smell of jasmine was thick and sweet. Annie Mason rang to say she and Arnold couldn't come because it was too hot.

'Bizarre. Over ninety and still going up and you know what Arnold's like in the heat.' Bitty slammed down the receiver and went back to the terrace clutching her dress at the midriff like a mediaeval queen. Either she'd shrunk or it had dropped, because even in high heels, which were killing her, it drooped in great swags in front.

'It really is too bad, letting people down at the last moment.' And how typical of Annie to state the obvious. Of course it was hot. Everyone knew it was hot, especially her, sweating already in the chiffon kaftan. A horrible mistake, even if it did hide the bulges and give rather a regal air, or was it lunar? After three gins Bitty didn't give a hoot whether Arnold and Annie came or not. Probably better that they didn't, Desmond would have found them very provincial. That was if he came. He'd said he'd come and was charming about it. What a pity it wasn't just the two of them having a nice, civilised little dinner at the cool Reina Christina, sitting in comfortable rattan chairs instead of Jimmy's rackety bar, and the manager telling her how long it was since she'd dropped in and how much they missed her. It was always good to be seen to be appreciated by the locals. Unnerved by the lack of jollity, she crunched the last ice cubes in her drink and stared irritably at the spread-out little group. Titus, sulking at the far end of the terrace with that Walkman thing blocking him off. Minou and Ingrid, thick as thieves and that brother of Jimmy's, surly fellow for all that he was in television. Which reminded her, she must ask him if he knew David Attenborough. Pity Jimmy hadn't come, at least he had a spark of life but someone had to deal with the dinner. It was so quiet. Parties were meant to be fun. They always used to be fun.

'Titus, why don't you turn that thing up so we can all hear?' He was leaning on the balustrade listening to soundtracks from Cody's films which Minou had given him for his birthday. Big swerving music which made him feel heroic. He'd need to be a hero tonight and he was only trying because he'd promised Minou he'd be good.

'Think of it as an initiation,' she'd said, laughing. He'd resisted painting red-and-black stripes on his face and dressed in white from head to toe instead. A young prince was the effect he had in mind, even if every instinct told him he should be a warrior, ready and waiting to decapitate that dreadful Desmond Macmahon with one sweep of a machete. That was what you did to people who stole your home.

'The boy's deaf,' grumbled Bitty. Typical to throw a mood on his birthday when everyone had gone to so much trouble. Ungrateful little pig. Even when she gave him three windsurfing T-shirts at breakfast he had just glanced in the bag and dropped it on the table.

'Juanita! More ice! Now, where was I?' With a half trip she plopped down again beside Tom on the wicker sofa.

'The pirate,' Tom prompted her politely. Trapped between gusts of Jolie Madame and the farting dogs, he dearly wished he'd followed his gut instinct and stayed with Jimmy to polish glasses. He tried to shift but was blocked by the dogs lying as dead, except the Peke who was drooling frothy saliva over his shoe.

'Oh yes, the pirate. Cody was quite a pirate in his own way, you know.' Bitty treated him to a vivacious whinny.

'A legend.' His murmur was automatic. Unable to bear it any longer he rose on the pretext of refilling his glass and wiped his shoe on the back of his trouser leg. Bitty ordered him to look at the view. He obeyed.

'They used to row out, plunder away . . .' Tom withdrew his gaze from the hazy sea and glanced down at Minou and Ingrid, gently submissive to the heat, chatting on the steps. Minou looked different, he thought.

'And your sister? Was Cody her father?' He interrupted the bit about buried treasure.

'Yes,' conceded Bitty in a voice which implied 'who knows?' The information worried Tom. He liked the story about the mother in Martinique and the dress shop and this demystification somehow spoiled the excitement of knowing so little. And she was wearing a dress. Pity, he'd got used to that tablecloth thing even though he had to admit it was a very pretty dress. Ingrid looked different, too. For one thing she was laughing. She'd washed her pale hair which stood prettily around her head. In the evening light they looked like flowers, a white tulip and a tiger lily. He pulled himself together, putting such idiotic fancy down to the full moon.

'What time is it?' Bitty dabbed powder on her pink face. Still no sign of Desmond. She strained to hear his car. A Rolls, probably. The dogs weren't much help. Usually they could hear a car at the end of the drive, but they were so far gone with heat they wouldn't notice if it ran over them. Oh, if he didn't show up she'd die. But he said he'd come and surely a man of such breeding would never just not show up.

'When do you think I should give him this?' Ingrid asked Minou, pulling an envelope tied with silver ribbon from her bag. She'd spent all day worrying about whether to give it to Titus when they were alone or casually when she arrived but hadn't done either. To give it to him intimately might be too . . . well, too intimate. Just because they'd done it didn't give her cause for assuming too much. She told herself this over and over again. Her friends at university did it all the time and never thought twice. But then, they'd never done it with a god.

'What is it?' Minou asked gently. Ingrid blushed and shrugged.

'Nothing much.' It was a pitiful attempt to be offhand. Minou wondered, not for the first time that evening, if something had happened. If it hadn't, it was about to. Twisting around, she beckoned Titus with an elegant brown arm. Ingrid whipped off her granny specs and put them in her bag, blinking in anticipation and nerves. She'd tried the contact lenses and lost one in seconds; she suspected it was lost somewhere behind her right eye.

'I wonder if it's too dark for 100 ASA?' After a blurred rummage in her bag she produced a camera and two films. 'I think it is.' She concentrated on winding a faster film on to the sprockets.

'Hullo,' said Titus pleasantly and sat down between them on the steps.

'Give it to him now, Ingrid,' Minou advised in a wicked stage whisper. Staring into total blackness through the lens, because she'd forgotten to take off the cap, Ingrid handed the envelope to Titus. He opened it, a blue card with wild flowers delicately arranged in a perfect circle. At the top she'd written in neat, schoolgirlish writing, 'To Titus, with love from the Mountain of Light.' It seemed all right when she wrote it but now she prayed he wouldn't think it gushy. You never knew with Titus.

He cleared his throat and said in a voice that Minou had never heard before, 'Thank you.' He put his arm round Ingrid's thin shoulder and planted a kiss somewhere near her ear. Her large, round eyes shone with joy. It was like watching an iceberg melt. Tactfully, Minou rose and joined Tom on the terrace.

'To young love,' she said, raising her glass: 'I hope.'

'Desmond! At last! How sweet of you to come!' Arms outstretched, Bitty sailed towards him like a midnight blue Valkyrie as he made his entrance quietly. Cool, impeccable, in beautifully ironed grey and carrying an unwrapped leatherbound book.

'Oh, you shouldn't have.' Bitty eyed the book, thinking how chic it was not to wrap it and wondering if it was a first edition. Desmond managed to stop her wrenching it from his hand.

'Juanita! The tapas!' His arrival should have been heralded with loud trumpet music. Juanita slapped out from the kitchen with cocktail bits on a silver tray, wearing her black dress and an even blacker expression. She hadn't put on an apron and hadn't changed her shoes. Bitty looked daggers at the broken, plastic sandals, rose above it and fussed around the drinks table, looking for ice in a bucket of tepid water. She located the Champagne tucked behind the other bottles. French, seventeen quid a bottle at Safeway's, and she'd be damned if the others were going to get at it.

'Just a little family party.' She handed Desmond a sparkling glass. 'This is Tom Fox from London, he's in TV, and this is my half-sister, Josephine Latour.' Nobody made a move. In a masterpiece of dismissal, Desmond appeared not to have heard Tom's name or even noticed he was there. Tom did likewise as he fought the mad idea that Desmond, intent on more destruction, had followed him like a menace from a bad dream. Minou looked quickly from one man to the other and the Jack Russell snapped awake and started growling.

'Oh, you naughty boy.' Bitty shoved him under the sofa with her foot and propelled Minou towards Desmond's outstretched hand and overstretched smile.

'So clever, our Josephine, works for all the top couture houses. PR or something, isn't it?' said Bitty, who couldn't think for the life of her what Minou had said she did. For a moment she considered assuring Desmond, forcing Minou to assure Desmond, that all the legalities with Entrail would be finalised tomorrow, then remembered it wasn't done to talk business at a party.

'I don't think we've met,' said Desmond, who knew they had, but to his intense irritation couldn't place her.

Oh yes we have, thought Minou grimly. We've met. A long time back, a rainy evening at Madame's when he arrived with one of the directors of the Louvre. Madame was having a rest and Minou was receiving for her. Which meant being polite, charming, talking about the weather, offering Champagne and tactfully discovering what the gentlemen had in mind. But Madame didn't rest easy for long. Shortly after Desmond had been taken upstairs by Babette, one of the most sophisticated of the girls, there was a commotion. Babette appeared on the landing, screaming, her cheek bloodied.

'*Non! Non! Non! Mais non!*' Madame, wrapped in a vast, turquoise cardigan, scurried up the stairs and had an urgent, whispered word with the distraught girl then turned on Desmond like a tiger.

'*Sortez!*' she cried, bundling him down the stairs, '*Sortez, et prenez votre parapluie avec!*'

'What happened?' asked the astonished Minou.

'Never you mind,' retorted Madame and returned to her room, muttering dark things about Les Anglais and the Nazis.

Desmond was looking at Minou as if she was a clue in the *Times* crossword. He asked if it was her first visit to La Preciosa and how long she was staying. He'd heard from Norman Trail there was a reluctance on her part to sign. She hesitated, knowing without doubt that he had a distant memory of her. Not that she had anything to hide, anything to be ashamed of, but she was deeply aware that Tom, less than three feet away and his back turned, was listening to every word. If ever the two of them reached a time to talk, of history, of dreams and maybe futures, she wanted to do it her own way. Nothing was ever what it seemed and whatever fragile beginnings she'd had she wasn't going to let Desmond destroy them by announcing he'd met her in a brothel in Paris.

'Yes, this is my first visit,' she said primly then added she wasn't staying long. She was going to sail away to Martinique. But she didn't tell him that. He asked her where she lived and like an idiot she said Paris. She turned away from Desmond and stood by Tom.

'How's the *Dancing Lady*?' she asked.

'Hush!' Tom panicked. A mere whisper of the boat in front of Desmond might cause her to sink without a trace in the yacht club. Rather than explain, he left to have a pee. Instinctively Minou knew he was right to keep quiet and at the same time realised that nobody had mentioned the boat to anyone, not even Jimmy, who was the first to tell everybody everything. Maybe it was a sacred secret. Or, to be more realistic, the wisest course of action to stop hordes of people stowing away in an escape from the *bojeo*.

'Now, where is that birthday boy? Titus, come and say hullo to Desmond.' Titus abandoned Ingrid and bounded up the steps with boyish haste and a sweet expression. Desmond handed him the book with murmured congratulations. It was *Paradise Lost*. With murder in his heart, Titus flashed him a beautiful smile. Minou and Juanita exchanged a worried look. Juanita thrust the tapas tray into Minou's hands and hurried back to the kitchen muttering, 'Dark moon . . . no moon . . . bad moon.' Minou glanced up. It looked all right, round and silver, spotlighting the strange performance Titus was putting on for Desmond. He'd opened the book at random and started to read out loud:

> So talked the spirited sly snake: and Eve
> Yet more amaz'd unwarie thus reply'd
> Serpent, thy overpraising leaves in doubt
> the virtue of the fruit.

He read it in English beautifully then thanked Desmond very formally in Spanish and almost gave a little bow.

'He hasn't had his proper present from me yet,' Bitty chimed. 'But I always think it's better to let people choose, don't you?' At which point Tom returned, having splashed his head with cold water, having said to hell with Desmond Macmahon. He overheard Bitty's grande geste.

'What's it to be, Titus?' he asked cheerily.

'A motorbike,' was the demure reply.

'A what?' gasped Bitty.

'A Yamaha V-Max.' Titus looked at the moon as if he was asking it for the Holy Grail.

'Good choice,' said Tom and they started to talk about bikes. Minou turned away to hide her giggles and offered the tapas to Ingrid who was standing on a chair taking pictures at impossible angles. It was the inclination of her head, her outstretched arm, that jerked Desmond's memory back to the Rue St Supplice. And she'd admitted she lived in Paris. Well, well, well, so Miss Latour was one of the girls. Or had been. Not, he suspected, something she'd care to broadcast, particularly to that young idiot Fox. His radar hadn't missed the fractional half glance she'd made in his direction when she mentioned Paris. Just a word, a hint, that was all it would take to complete. She wasn't stupid.

'What did Juanita mean, "black moon"?' asked Ingrid, clambering down from the balustrade.

'Total eclipse, visible through its entirety, a rare phenomenon.' Since Bitty hadn't thought her worth introduction, Desmond answered her as if she were minor royalty.

'Oh dear.' She looked anxiously at the sky and checked

the light against the stone walls. 'Quickly, everyone, a family group, the light's going.'

'Cheese, everyone, cheese.' Bitty hustled everyone together in an awkward line, herself in the middle next to Desmond, who, in the spirit of things, put his arms around as many people as possible, especially Titus. Tom and Minou stared stonily at the camera. Bitty raised her glass and made a funny face.

'Cheese.' Ingrid clicked then asked Titus, 'One on your own, just you.' After all it was his birthday, and should he vanish like a dream she'd have something to remember him by. Titus posed attractively. She took a long time to frame him but the longer he gazed at the lens the more handsome he became. Tom noticed Desmond staring at the boy, his gaze sweeping over him then down on to the statue by the fountain, lingering just a fraction too long on the smooth, bronze buttocks.

'Oh, so that's it, you old queen,' he muttered. Tom, who had nothing against gays in general, nevertheless, turned away from Macmahon as if he'd witnessed something obscene.

'Right everyone, let's go, I'm starving. I do hope Jimmy's . . .' Bitty was about to say sober but thought better of it. 'Just pot-luck at the local bistro,' she apologised to Desmond, who intimated that pot-luck was the most delightful thing imaginable.

Ingrid, whose English didn't run to pot-luck, suspected that it was not nice. 'Jimmy's all right.' She defended him stoutly. He'd swept the patio, gone back into town to get cochineal for her to ice the cake and had to be stopped from ringing a restaurant in Hong Kong to get their secret recipe for sea-bass. Also, he and Tom had bought and paid for the lobster which, at three thousand pesetas a kilo, was very generous.

'Can I give anyone a lift?' offered Desmond.

'Oh, that would be lovely.' Bitty hitched up the garment and hurried up the drive to find out if it was a Rolls.

'Wait!' cried Minou. 'We haven't got a picture of Ingrid.' Ingrid fell into a bout of modest panic and said it didn't matter.

'Oh, but it does. I'll take it, you and Titus together.' She took the camera from Ingrid as if it was an object from an alien culture.

'It looks very professional,' she said dubiously.

It was all dials, like the cameras Jean Luc used for wars. He never took snapshots. He told her life was for living, not recording. It was strange that, from a man who took pictures of desolation for the world. Then he told her that for him, life meant her. And that explained why he never took a picture of her, not one.

'But I want a picture of you.' She had to plead with him until he relented and posed grumpily on the Pont Neuf.

'Why don't my pictures look like yours?' she complained when it came out all fuzzy. A technical explanation wasn't his way. He told her she wasn't concentrating.

'But I was.'

'No, you weren't. To see, you must *look*. Look at whatever it is as if it's the last thing you'll see before you die. Then you'll see it.' Maybe that was why his pictures tore people's hearts out. She often wondered what it was, that last thing he saw before he died. But she never knew because they never found his camera either.

She posed them against the balustrade, Ingrid so flower-like, so vulnerable, she almost trembled, and

Titus, tonight confident as a black cat. She breathed in and out a few times before she clicked.

'Oh, come on, you lot!' Bitty was overjoyed because of the Rolls.

'That'll be a nice one,' said Minou confidently, giving the camera back to Ingrid. She'd really looked. Ingrid wound off the film and put it in her bag.

'You coming?' called Tom, who was halfway across the yellow lawn to the short-cut. Ingrid ran down the steps to join him and started crashing through the bamboo like a noisy deer.

'Coming?' he called again to Minou, his tone owning her, as if she had been his for a long, long time.

'A bit oppressive to walk, don't you think?' Desmond was at her side. He took her elbow and glanced at her feet. She'd forgotten she was wearing high heels. She shook her head for Tom and reluctantly followed Desmond towards the drive. Tom gave a 'no matter' shrug and followed Ingrid, but stopped suddenly and did a double take. There was something about the statue in the garden. Something. Perhaps it moved.

'Can I come in the car too? Can I sit in the front?' Titus smiled at Desmond even more beautifully as he opened the back door of the Rolls for Minou. She gave him a shove in the chest.

'Titus, what are you up to?' she hissed.

'Nothing,' he said innocently. 'Just trailing the cape.'

'It's a going concern,' Jimmy assured Desmond and offered him a cigar. Desmond gave half a glance around El Snitos, which Ingrid had transformed.

'Overdoing it a bit? Looks like a tart's bedroom,' Jimmy had said to her, worried about fire regulations. Pink crêpe paper hung in ballooning swags from the ceiling, draped the walls and looped over the doors ending in fat, pink bows centred with bunches of corn. Ingrid assured him it was a Very Old Swedish Custom to bandage everything in sight with coloured paper on festive occasions.

'Very popular with the locals.' Jimmy persevered with Desmond as a fleet of noisy revellers sped past to the Feria. As if to prove him right Bonker arrived, followed by Bonquette, and for the first time in memory both sat down at the bar. Bonquette had abandoned her sombre colours and wore flame red, a fringed shawl and a carnation anchored in her oil-black hair. Jimmy gave them their usual. Neither of them made a move to retire to the car-park.

'Too hot for it, then?' asked Jimmy with a wink which was beyond Bonker, but Bonquette, getting the gist, fanned herself with a big sparkly fan. Jimmy asked if they were going to the Feria. Bonquette, with the expression of a large Cinderella, looked away. Bonker looked at his shoes, shook his head then appeared to count the bubbles in his drink. Eventually he raised his glass to the pink garlands.

'*Muy bonito*,' he said.

'Jimmy,' called Bitty, tormented by the idea that he was quite capable of asking he pair to join their table. 'So colourful, don't you think?' she asked Desmond, covering herself in case he did. 'Jimmy, have you told Desmond?' Her words were lost in the klaxon of a police car or ambulance on the main road. Jimmy, who thought Bitty meant the one about the three nuns and the astronaut, clapped Bonker on the back.

'Well, you see, there were these three nuns . . .' Minou had heard the joke before from a boy at Hastings High when she was fourteen. At least she thought she had but Jimmy, flushed with being centre stage, muffed the punch line, repeated it, laughed and started off again.

'Well you see, there were these three nuns . . .' Bitty hooted because he had beer froth on his nose. Desmond gave an uncommitted smile. Ingrid, who was drunk for the first time in her life, had trouble following it the first time and wondered why he was saying it all over again. She still didn't understand it. Titus, who had taken the precaution of nibbling on a little Datura root in the Rolls, was just beginning to feel omnipotent and assumed an expression of benign dignity. Minou looked at Tom at the far end of the table to see his reaction. He hadn't spoken to her throughout the meal or to anyone else except Ingrid and the goat. He kept quietly out of the mainstream, clearing away lobster debris, setting clean plates and glasses and leaving Jimmy to make a triumphant entry with the sea-bass. He didn't laugh at the joke, just gave a quick head-ducking movement to shake it away. Real men, Minou found herself thinking, didn't tell or laugh at dirty jokes. As if to laugh would reduce the magic of the real thing. It was another message, another point of recognition and for her it gave an intangible feeling of relief.

'What do you do? Where do you go?' Ingrid asked dreamily and gazed through the trellis as if the answer to her question lay behind the stars in the hot, black sky. She got up and put on a flamenco tape.

'Olé!' shouted Jimmy and told Bonker and Bonquette to help themselves to drinks and chalk it on the board.

Desmond leaned towards Titus. 'Do you ever come to the *corrida* in Seville?' He'd looked into the story of the Great Manolo.

'No,' said Titus sweetly, realising the old fart had done his homework.

'You're not an *aficionado*?' Desmond feigned surprise.

Titus said he wasn't and left it to him as to what could have gone wrong with his DNA coding. 'Not too keen on bloodshed and all that.' He used his best public school voice.

Bitty beamed at them both. They were getting on so well. It was really kind of Desmond to take such an interest and it would be so wonderful if maybe he offered Titus a job. Something simple at the bodega, rolling sherry barrels or something. Titus could stay put and she could go back to blissful Wiltshire and everyone would be happy. As long as Titus stayed being nice. He was quite capable of being as normal as anyone else when he tried.

'Youth, ah, youth,' said Desmond, turning to Minou. 'It has so much to teach us, don't you think?'

'Not really,' she replied coldly, still fired with the spirit of Madame and ready to contradict everything this dreadful, creepy man said.

'Whatever they know, whatever they've learned, we're always one step further down the road learning something new.' She stubbed out her cigarette. New things, like owning half a house you didn't want and trying to make the right decision. Like trying not to loathe Bitty, tonight so filled with manic energy and hormone therapy. And worse, trying not to feel again. Madame knew, Madame tried to tell her so often: passion leads to trouble. But this wasn't something new, just something she'd forgotten. She looked at Tom and then away, warding off definable reasons for being drawn.

'Happy birthday to you . . .' Ingrid paused in the doorway with the cake, her face aglow, the light of the twenty-one candles reflected in her granny specs. With deepest reverence she put the cake on the table in front of Titus. It was very large, of indeterminate shape and also swathed in pink crêpe paper.

'. . . Happy birthday to you.'

Titus blew out the candles in one. Everyone clapped and Jimmy started a ribald version of 'Twenty-One Today'.

'Speech! Speech!' Titus shook his head, which wasn't to say he hadn't rehearsed several versions while dressing, but decided against it. They'd had an extract from *Paradise Lost* and it didn't do to spread oneself too thin. He gazed around the table at those he supposed were his nearest and dearest, all filmed in sweat. Poor Bitty, one had to feel sorry for the silly cow for having such a rotten way of looking at life. And Minou, who looked so tired, lonely and confused. Jimmy, who'd given him his first beer when he was ten years old; and that funny bloke from London was all right, or would be if he'd loosen up a bit. For a moment he was sidetracked by the idea of laying a little Datura on Tom later. Then there was Ingrid, almost crystal, gazing at him with heavy Nordic adoration. Of course it was only right that she should, but in a way, Titus admitted to himself, he hoped it wasn't solely because of him. And then again in a way he did. Then he glanced at Desmond. With every initiation there is a final test. Something horrible that sneaks up from the vile things writhing around in the unconscious, something unnamed to be, if not conquered, at least controlled. The test tonight was obviously Desmond, who was staring at him like a cobra. Titus closed his eyes and called on the Datura to deal with it, to turn the man into a speck of light and vanish, like turning off a TV. He opened his eyes.

Desmond, the grey suit, the smile and the well cut hair were gone. His chair was empty. Titus gave a deep sigh of satisfaction, picked up the knife and plunged it into the cake which turned out to be pink on the inside as well.

'Make a wish!' they all cried.

He shook his head with suitable modesty. 'I have everything.'

Minou looking at him, so young, so brave, so funny and sad, tended to agree but to be on the safe side closed her eyes and made a wish for him. Bonker and Bonquette raised their glasses.

'Come on over,' called Jimmy.

'Told you he would,' muttered Bitty.

Bonker and Bonquette refused with stately diffidence. Jimmy turned up the music.

Bonquette snapped her fan shut and like a magnificent queen descended from her barstool. She raised her shawl above her head, tied it firmly round her hips and with a swaying movement crossed the space between the bar and the table and stopped in front of Titus. He looked up at her, and pulled by her intent, rose to his feet.

'Oh my God.' Horrified, Bitty realised they were going to dance. Her son was about to make a fool of himself and she was going to die of embarrassment. She looked at Desmond, now back again, who didn't seem to mind in the least, then back at Titus who was staring into the face of that dreadful woman. Not a feature alive except their eyes, Titus's bright and glittering, giving as good as he was getting from Bonquette's blazing glance of near disdain. She gave a little snake-like twist of her wrists and clattered her heels. Titus took his stance and raised his arms. If this was the Ultima Madre he could deal with it. Tom marvelled at his cool.

'Bravo, Titus,' breathed Minou, amazed that her rather incoherent wish for him was coming true so soon.

'Go for it, lad!' shouted Jimmy and turned the volume up. Bonker started to slap out a rhythm, familiar as a religious habit, on the bar with the flat of his big hand.

'*Olé!*' cried Ingrid faintly. For Bitty there was only one way out. Mumbling something about the little girls' room and taking care to loop the droopy skirt over her arm she headed for the door where she stopped and, just for the hell of it, managed a skittish little twirl of her own which no one noticed. Titus and Bonquette circled, advanced, retreated, spurned, turned again and challenged. The blunt, crude music began to seep into Tom's bones. He'd never listened to flamenco before, not to the sounds, and to his surprise he felt a pang of envy for the lamenting singer for being so very sure of being so sad. He looked at Minou, her face cupped in her hands, aglow with admiration for the dancing boy. There was no sadness there.

In the Ladies, Bitty made do with a bit of crisp lavatory paper. There were no towels, not even one of those soggy roller things. She stared at herself in the flyblown mirror. The light was awful and she looked eau-de-Nil in colour. Oh, for a little drink at the Reina Christina. She snapped her bag shut, hitched up the dress and made for the door. It was time to leave the 'young people' alone to enjoy themselves. Desmond would understand and, galling as it was to include Minou among the young, three was definitely a crowd. Bitty started back to the bar, all plans made, then stopped with an abrupt 'Oh!' In the silent moonlight a group of men were standing in the drive. Six of them, obviously Spanish. There was another group, all women, with black shawls draped over their heads. Unnerved by their sinister stillness, Bitty quickened her step but they didn't seem to notice her. She glanced back and to her dismay recognised the tallest of the men. Five foot four if an inch, one of The Great Manolo's brothers, that horrible man who'd sneered at her in the hotel suite in Seville, twenty-one years, nine months ago. Oh, she'd never forget that face.

'Don't run,' Bitty told herself. 'Whatever you do, don't run.'

Titus and Bonquette, with great sweat stains under their arms, were still stamping away. Desmond continued to watch them. Bitty stopped by his chair and fanned herself with a beer mat.

'I'm terribly sorry to be a party poop but I've got a splitting headache.' Desmond inclined his head to hear above the music. Bitty said it all again, not easy to sound fragile if one had to shout, but all hell was going to break out, she knew it in her bones. So humiliating. Desmond grasped what she was saying and with no to-do rose and took her arm. Out of the corner of her eye, Bitty saw that the Spaniards were now standing in the doorway, their arms folded across their chests. Desmond turned back and leaned over Minou's chair.

'I'll send the car for you tomorrow. About nine?'

'Car?' She couldn't think what he was talking about.

'Mr Trail,' he reminded her.

'Oh, *come* on.' Bitty lost her head and beckoned wildly.

'Thank you.' He left no room for discussion, turned and left with Bitty. Minou looked down at her hands, all the joy drained from her. Tom moved into Desmond's empty seat.

'Anything wrong?' He hoped she'd tell him what the man had said, what it was that caused her abrupt change of mood. He broke off as he noticed the Spaniards. 'What the hell?'

The man in front of the group got straight down to business and pulled out a stiletto. It landed with a nasty thunk in the bar and quivered next to Bonker's gin and tonic. Bonker removed his hand and with a great sense of the appropriate switched off the tape. Bonquette stamped to a halt and stood like a haughty tree in the middle of the floor. Jimmy's smile of welcome faded. The Spaniards pushed him aside and advanced as one upon Bonker. One of them smashed a bottle. Bonquette screamed and threw herself towards him like a deranged tiger. One of the Spanish women let out a shrill shout and poked a skinny finger at her. The others set up a chant of insults which included the words whore, adulteress and cuckold.

'*Caramba,*' drawled Titus and did the first thing that came to mind. Putting on a tape of 'Carmen', he thoughtfully removed a few glasses from the bar. All movement was suspended as the challenge of Bizet's overture throbbed out.

'Titus! You must be mad.' Minou flew across the room and turned off the tape. One of the Spanish women spat at her.

'I say!' Jimmy was outraged. Suddenly everyone was lunging, shuffling and shouting. Four of the little men leaped on Bonker who fended them off with great sweeps of his burly arms. With a screeching and shaking of fists the women egged the men on. The little lady from the fish-market hopped in and out of the melée acting as the umpire.

'Can't have this. Put 'em up, sir, put 'em up.' Jimmy danced around making little jabs at the air with his fists.

'I shouldn't do that,' Tom advised. He'd got to his feet and was quietly assessing how many they were up against and what was likely to happen. A bottle flew through the air and crashed near Minou and Ingrid.

'What is going on?' asked Ingrid who'd lost her specs again and had the first tremors of a hangover.

'Under,' Tom grabbed them and pushed them towards the table.

'Under,' Ingrid repeated this thoughtfully. 'In Spanish, *abajo*.'

'*Abajo* then.' He shoved them under and turned to Jimmy still jabbing and prancing.

'What's happening?' Ingrid asked again as Minou lifted up the edge of the tablecloth on to a copse of thick legs in black stockings, pointed patent shoes and dusty boots. Jimmy's Reeboks jumped in and out of spaces and Tom's plimsolls were everywhere at once. She lifted the cloth further. The goat, bleating in terror, was rushing round butting knees. Titus was leaning on the bar smoking a cheroot.

'Bonker, watch it!' shouted Jimmy. Titus swept up the goat and covered its eyes so it wouldn't be frightened as three of the little men prepared to hurl Bonker from the bar. Jimmy grabbed an impacted blue chair. It wouldn't budge. There was a nasty wrenching sound.

'Oh shit, my arm.' He gasped, and fell to the floor clutching his shoulder. Minou crawled out from under the table towards him.

'Get back!' Tom shouted as another bottle crashed against the wall. She huddled back against Ingrid. There was a new pair of feet, familiar feet in broken turquoise plastic sandals planted firmly apart. The hubbub died down. The boots and patent shoes came to a standstill and shuffled about. The owner of the turquoise sandals was obviously giving everybody hell.

'It's Juanita.' Minou recognised the voice. 'What's she saying?'

Ingrid translated in rapid monotone.

'They ought to be ashamed of themselves.' She listened carefully to the torrent. 'That Titus, being who he is, will bring the wrath of the Virgin Mary down on the lot of them for having disrupted the day of his manhood.'

'Bravo!' Minou came out from under the table again. Juanita, hands on hips, hadn't finished. The son of The Great Manolo Torero, Torero, Torero, deserved more respect than to be put in danger by his own kith and kin. As far as Minou could make out, Juanita's darling was enjoying every moment of it. Juanita stepped over the inert Jimmy and held up Titus's arm. Affected by this temporary deification, the Spaniards gazed with dawning understanding.

'Niño! Tesoro!' One of the women in black tottered to Titus and fell upon him with open arms.

'Mi nieto, mi nieto.'

'Nieto?' queried Minou.

'Grandson,' explained Ingrid, who'd joined her and was pushing a cushion under Jimmy's head. 'Yes, must be; *abuela*, that means grandmother.' Juanita came to her finale by rounding on Bonquette for being no better than she ought but after a quick glance at the cuckolded husband added that perhaps it was understandable. This brought a spasm of indignation from one of the women, his mother. But the rumpus went no further as all eyes turned to Mona, Entrail's Secretary, who arrived, in flashing white high heels and a twelve-inch miniskirt.

'Jimmeee . . .' She gave a cry of dismay and threw herself on to the floor beside him.

'Oh, it's you, Mona,' said Jimmy and fainted thankfully into her arms.

No one noticed Bonker's lonely departure except Bonquette, who was held back by a flurry of black arms and fringed shawls and frog-marched to her father-in-law's car. It was decided she wasn't fit to go to the Feria. As the car made for the main road she looked wistfully out of the back window at the space beneath the eucalyptus tree where the Peugeot had shaken for the last time.

'Do you need a hand?' Tom asked Mona as they lowered Jimmy on to the back seat of her Metro. Mona assured him that she didn't, that she had a cousin who worked nights at the clinic and anyway the nuns were as strong as horses. She settled herself, started up and backed round the Spaniards who were slapping each other on the back and arguing about who would drive Titus and the Señorita to the Feria. Honour avenged, Bonquette's husband took Titus by the arm and started to recite Lorca.

'*Aqui, amigo, aqui.*' Titus deliberated between lift offers and chose the car most suitable to his status. He ushered Ingrid into the back of an old Chevrolet. The sleepy goat slung over one shoulder, he turned for a moment and looked at Minou. She was standing in the doorway of the wrecked bar next to Tom. He looked again very carefully. A pink crêpe figure-of-eight hanging above their heads seemed to loop them together. Bit like a bride and groom on top of a cake. Titus shrugged. No accounting for taste. Tom was a nice enough chap, he supposed, and as long as Minou was happy it was all right with him. He resisted giving them the sign of the cross and climbed into the Chevrolet beside Ingrid.

Minou straightened up with an armful of pink paper and stuffed it into a plastic bag.

'Look out for broken glass.' It was the first thing he'd said in half and hour. He was sweeping up the chaos into a neat pile where Titus and Bonquette had stamped and sidled round each other. His shirt was splattered with red wine, his hair rumpled and he didn't look English any more.

'You've torn your dress,' he remarked and looked briefly at her brown thigh through the ripped silk. She bent down for more paper. He went on sweeping with long, unfussy strokes.

'What's with you and Desmond Macmahon?' he asked, poking under a blue chair for an evasive bit of broken bottle.

'Nothing.' Minou turned from scraping fish-bones off a plate into the garbage pail. 'He's sending a car for me at nine.' Tom glanced at the watch on his wrist.

'Why?' They moved slowly, fluently, stepping round each other, back and forth between the carnage on the table to the pantry and the sink as she told him about the house, about the will, about Bitty and about her father. Sometimes she was hesitant, as if recounting the history of a foreign race almost impossible to understand. He asked her no questions and made no interruptions as he swilled the glasses round in soapy water, rinsed them under a running tap and set them one by one in neat rows on the draining-board.

'Tomorrow it will all be over.' She flicked away some crumbs and folded a tea-towel into a neat square, walked to the sink and stood beside him rinsing her hands under the tap. He was rolling down his sleeves and buttoning his cuffs. The buttons were tiny, mother of pearl gleaming against the blue cotton. The cicadas had stopped and it was very quiet. She could feel waves of warmth from his body and almost hear the sound of his heart above her own. They listened for a moment.

'Do you think it's because of the full moon?' she asked him.

'Probably.' His head was bent and his voice was almost inaudible. She made no decision, there was no urgency of choice as her hands moved to the back of his head, her fingers sliding through his strong hair then down his temples where they fluttered gently across his closed eyes and on until they reached the tiny, top button of his shirt. He opened his eyes and smiled and reached through the torn dress for her thigh. Without haste or clumsy fumbling their clothes fell on the newly swept floor. The hardness, almost roughness of his palms surprised her skin and then delighted her as he swept them from her shoulder blades, down her pliant back to her waist. She was no longer fragile or elusive and all his half-wonderings dissolved with certainty.

They lay on Jimmy's crumpled bed under the open window and closed in on each other. His cry of exaltation flew up into the dark night. She lay back, filled and steady, sleek in her contentment. With the seal of secrets broken they talked with the ease of those who reach the short-cut home after a long journey. Outside, the sharp edge of the moon had been shadowed out in a clean bite.

'Have you ever been to Martinique before?' she asked him.

CHAPTER TEN

THE ROLLS WAS already parked beneath the fig tree as Minou walked slowly up the drive, the pressure of Tom's goodbye touch still warm upon her shoulder. The Peke advanced to meet her, gasping like a messenger with painful tidings.

'Ah, there you are.' Bitty, in her housecoat, was standing by the car. She'd decided to be terrifyingly nice, not to say a word about people who stayed out all night. She had her way, others had theirs. She'd scraped her hair back from her face, scrubbed it free of all make-up until it shone. Natural and nice. Desmond, although reluctant to have a nightcap at the Reina Christina, had been absolutely sweet, suggesting that she (and Titus) might have lunch at the bodega sometime soon.

'The car's been here for ages,' she said, which wasn't strictly true. Minou stared at her as if she were a rude stranger intruding on the silence which had cocooned her since she and Tom had woken, loved, lain and at last reluctantly detached.

'Oh? Where's Desmond?' she asked vaguely.

'He sent the chauffeur.' Bitty hadn't been able to decide if this was a step up or a step down. 'Holt!

Holt!' Holt, the chauffeur, came out of the kitchen where he had been given a cup of tea. He stubbed out his cigarette and put on his grey peaked cap. Bitty handed him a bit of paper on which she'd printed Norman Trail's address and number in large capitals. Her explanations of Gibraltar's one way system round Library Street were cut short by one of the labradors lunging past her.

'Oh, a rat! A rat! You clever girl! *Venga, venga, venga*!' The black animal yelped and jumped her bulk about in the bushes.

'Aren't you going to change?' She noticed the rip in Minou's dress, then could have bitten her tongue off. What did it matter what she looked like for Entrail as long as she got there. *Now*! Minou shook her head. Later, she'd shower and sing, put on fresh clothes and collect her few belongings. Until then, when all reason for her presence at La Preciosa was null and void, Tom's smell upon her body would protect her like a talisman. Holt opened the door of the car and gave her a quick up and down look.

'Got your passport?' Bitty fussed alongside as he closed Minou in the air-conditioned cell.

Bitty went back to the house and made herself hot water and lemon. She took a sip, grimaced, looked at her watch and rang Entrail. He wasn't there yet, they told her, but he was expected any minute.

'Miss Latour is on her way.' They replied, yes, she was expected as well. Jubilant, Bitty put down the receiver and retied the sash of her housecoat. To her delight the labrador waddled in with the rat drooping from its mouth.

'Oh, what a clever girl!' She caressed its ears, relieved

it of its trophy and chucked it in the bin outside the back door for Juanita to deal with. That was if she ever deigned to show up again.

'My God it's hot!' The fan was little help, blasting like a hair dryer.

'A drinkie, a little drinkie is what we all need.' The sweet, sharp taste of gin and Schweppes fizzed in her mouth. She knew it was very naughty, but after all a celebration is a celebration. However, she told herself severely, fair is fair. Since she'd cheated with a drink, she'd better have some of that disgusting diuretic stuff to cancel it out.

As soon as they reached the main road Holt took off his cap and laid it on the seat beside him.

'Hot, isn't it, Madam?' His tone was insolent and Minou noticed he had a boil on the back of his neck. And he was wrong, the air conditioning was chilling her until goosepimples stood out on her arms. She gave the briefest of nods, to quarantine herself from anything to do with Desmond. After a lifetime of experience, Holt had been quick to size up that his passenger wasn't what he'd call Real Class. He also came to the conclusion that being a Hottentot it was quite likely that she didn't speak English. Nevertheless, to punish her, he lapsed into an offended silence which lasted eight kilometres, until the first traffic lights on the outskirts of Algeciras. An army truck drew up alongside. The soldier driving it was about twenty, with olive skin and Latin eyes. He glanced down at the silver flanks of the Rolls with interest, then at Holt, his expression turning to dismissal. The lights were slow to change. Minou pressed a button and the window slid down with a discreet hum. The soldier looked at her and smiled. She smiled back, their eyes colluding in a lightning joke about the car – to hell with Holt. The soldier put on a cassette of Paco de Lucia. The lights changed to green and the two vehicles moved forward. The lingering vibration of the guitar hovered in the air, the real warm air from outside the car.

'Stop!' The music was a call from Titus. Titus whom Minou felt she'd abandoned in her happiness and left waving at her from a rock on a far shore, as she sailed away.

'Stop!' Holt stiffened, his neck bristled and appeared not to have heard. She wondered if he'd been told this might happen.

'I have to make a phone call.' She glanced out of the rear window at a retreating billboard for the Reina Christina.

'Take me to the Reina Christina.' Holt, mollified that at least it was a five-star hotel, though whether they'd let her in was another matter, did a reluctant turn and swept up the avenue of tall palms.

'I won't be a moment.' Before he had time to move Minou hopped out and slammed the door, something that in his memory had never ever happened, but then what could you expect? Unrepentant, brimming with her idea, she almost danced up the marble steps into the hotel.

The Reina Christina was built in the early part of the century when grand hotels were grand hotels. Swathed in rococo splendour, like a rich grandmother, the hotel had conceded with reluctance to modern necessities such as swimming pools; theirs glinted discreetly outside behind banks of oleander and hibiscus. The marble terrace looked out over the yacht club. Minou skipped across what had once been a ballroom, a gleaming parquet space below a massive chandelier.

At the far end was a mirrored bar, glass-topped tables, wicker chairs with snow-white linen covers. A barman was already dancing with his cocktail shakers. Several smaller rooms led off the ballroom, with chintz covered easy chairs and sofas, widely spaced for muted conversation over tea. As Minou had hoped, there was a writing room. On a Louis Quinze table, sat a blotter. She opened it and found some heavy writing paper emblazoned with a crown. She sat down. A waiter was at her side in a flash. She ordered a Buck's Fizz and borrowed his Biro.

> Dear Mr Trail,
> I, Josephine Marguerite Latour, do hereby abdicate . . .

She paused, wondering if abdicate was too royal. Her mind had flashed to a film of Cody's, one in which a Balkan queen was forced at gun point to give up her throne. It was a bit much. She crossed out abdicate. The page now looked a mess, so she took another piece of paper.

> Dear Mr Trail,
> I, Josephine Marguerite Latour, do hereby renounce all rights whatsoever in all and any claim to the said property La Preciosa as left to me by my late father. I wish to allocate those same rights to my half-nephew, Titus Nolan. I would be grateful if you, with the power vested in you . . .

She stopped again, but decided to let it pass.

> . . . would hereby act under these instructions and accept Power of Attorney on my behalf and

sign whatever documents you deem necessary in accordance with these my wishes.
Yours sincerely,
Josephine Marguerite Latour
P.S. Forthwith.

She added the date, looked up at a sunburst clock, added the time and took a cooling draught of Buck's Fizz. It was done.

The mystery was – why hadn't she thought of it before? Titus was a man now. He'd been acclaimed successor to his father, a hero, and had accepted this acclaim. Unearned homage was all very well but it didn't build character. Although he'd never fight a bull, the time had come to prove himself worthy in another arena and if ever there was a deadly opponent, it was Bitty. With half the house his legal right, they could fight to the death. *Oui, c'est juste.* Minou addressed the envelope to Norman Trail, wondering if she should have had witnesses. But any document written in clear intent was legally binding. (Cody, *The Dreyfuss Case* with Robert Donat.) She tipped the waiter a hundred pesetas and gave him back his Biro.

'Would you be kind enough to give this to the chauffeur and tell him to deliver it. Oh, and tell him I won't be needing him any more.' Giving Holt time to get clear, she finished her drink, then made her way to the lobby to ask the hall porter to get her a taxi.

The taxi-driver dropped her off on the main road at the bottom of the drive. He said he knew the house well and wasn't going to risk his new tyres on the pot-holes. She stood on the grass verge and watched him drive off towards Tarifa. There was no traffic to disturb the hot, flat silence. The sky was orange, the sun dull and it felt as if the earth was being grilled. Bitty was up there waiting to squeeze the living daylights out of her when she knew what she'd done. Minou fought back the impulse to run back to El Snitos and accept Tom's offer.

'Sure you don't want me to come with you?' he'd asked her earlier when she told him what she had to do. But she decided to forgo his chivalry. Together he and she were clean and new, not to be contaminated by the ugliness of what people did to one another. Just thinking of him, of his incisive honesty and generous heart, to say nothing of those wonderful hard-palmed hands, gave her courage. That, and the rightness of what she'd done, urged her into a steady pace across the road. The short-cut was out due to her high heels. Eyes down, nose dry, she kept going up the slope, picking her way delicately round pot-holes. The atmosphere pressed down on her and her dress stuck to her body. A dog howled. Another answered it, then other dogs from farms further up the hill began strange answers. If Norman Trail had phoned Bitty, as he was bound to, she'd already know, but allowing for the traffic Holt was probably delivering the letter at that moment. Which meant he'd ring while she was telling Bitty herself. Either way, it was going to be awful. The dogs stopped howling and there was silence. Suddenly it seemed vital to get to Bitty first, if not, there would be no honour and her gesture would be futile. Minou almost ran the last few yards towards the big green gates. They were still unoiled, stiff, firmly bolted against marauding Spanish hounds. She yanked the vertical bolt and tugged until, exasperated, she hurled herself against the bars.

Nothing. She reminded herself about mind over matter. Breathe in . . . breathe out . . . Bracing legs she grabbed the bars and shook them. The bolt began to quiver. She lurched to one side.

'*Merde*!' she glanced down to see if the heel of her shoe had snapped. Then she thought she might be fainting. Her head was clear but there was something wrong with her legs. With a creeping sense of dislocation she realised it was the ground beneath her. Ahead, in the drive, the tarmac burst upwards into a bubble. Minou clung to the gates as a deep groan sounded from the earth and turned into a roar. A stone shot past her and clanged against the metal bolts. The earth heaved, tipped her over, and threw her face down on the undulating gravel. She lay still for a moment, a curious excitement overtaking her, then fought her way to a kneeling position. Clinging to the gates, she wanted to shake them harder, as if to aid the anger of a lifetime being wrenched from her by the quaking earth. There was no way to tell how long it lasted. Then everything was still again. She looked up at the mountain and saw Titus halfway down, through a rolling dust, leaping across the scorched grass. Loosening her grip on the bars, Minou sat back on her heels, then froze in terror as a violent crack echoed over the *bojeo*. El Bueno was moving, rolling from side to side as if shaking his head. The great rock teetered for a moment on the ledge where it had rested since the earth cooled down. In slow motion it tipped, falling into the valley, flattening a tree and splintering off the outcrop of its nose and chin when it landed. Powerless, Minou watched the great skull as it began to roll towards the east wing of the house, slowly at first, as if not sure which way to go, then gathering speed, bouncing and bounding like a granite grapefruit towards the Range Rover directly in its path. It caught it on the engine, spinning it round like a Dinky Toy. A scream of splintering wood, crunching stone and shattering glass filled the air as it pounded through the pantry, bringing down the outer kitchen wall. And still it rolled, casually knocking over a telegraph pole, across the lawn until it at last came to rest in the bamboo grove where it broke into two big, unrepentant pieces. Minou stayed still. A tiny avalanche of pebbles trickled past her. Cautiously she rose and tested the ground beneath her. One side of the gate had broken from its hinges. She squeezed past.

'Bitty . . . Bitty . . .' She took off her shoes and started to run towards the house.

Titus, panting and covered in dust, arrived at the kitchen door as she stopped dead under the dangerously crooked lintel. The outer kitchen wall had fallen into a great pile of brick and stone, leaving the house open on to the greenhouse which had shattered into a great pile of gleaming glass. A beam above creaked and a rush of plaster fell around them in plate-sized chunks. They crouched, their arms over their heads. From somewhere came the sound of running water. A ghostly dust-covered labrador tried to clamber towards them.

'Sit!' ordered Minou, 'Sit.' Bewildered, it obeyed and waited for more orders. The beam slipped a bit more and then seemed to wedge itself. After a minute Minou decided to risk it.

'Bitty. Bitty . . .' She lowered her voice in case she brought down the sagging ceiling. Titus crawled toward the sideboard which had fallen on its side, scattering plates and recipes and tins of coffee. The phone swung by its cord. There was an appalling smell.

'Careful, there might be live wires,' he warned Minou

as she peered through a curtain of twisted cable and hanging wires.

'Or gas.'

'There isn't any,' he assured her. Minou stood up, her hands across her nose and mouth and peered through the haze of lifting, yellow grit. She could just make out the Jack Russell. It was licking something. A fat, white foot poking out from behind the kitchen table.

'Bitty?'

'Mum?' said Titus, his voice rising. 'Mum.' It was a name he hadn't used since he was six. Aghast, he looked back at Minou who nodded and went ahead of him. Bitty was lying on her back beside a broken bottle of Gordon's. She was in a pool of shit and vomit, her lips black, drawn into a dreadful smile and she was still clutching a teacup.

'Is she dead?' Titus asked when he could speak.

'Very.' Minou had to clear her throat before she said it. There was yellow slime trickling down Bitty's neck. Titus began to shake. Minou gagged. She was standing on a pile of vomit. The Jack Russell began to lick around her feet.

'Get out of here!' she yelled at it, not caring if she brought the house down. The dog cringed and slunk under the tipped-up kitchen sink. The body didn't appear to have been touched or injured by falling masonry or flying casseroles. She steeled herself, knelt down and took the teacup from Bitty's hand.

'It must have been a heart attack.' There was no pulse at all. In a puzzled daze Titus stared at his mother.

'Maybe.' He clasped his hands together to stop them shaking. 'But I think she took something. The silly cow took something.' He bent down and sniffed Bitty's mouth and pulled back from the acrid stench. Minou leaned against the sink to stop herself from being sick, turned on the tap but nothing happened.

'Give us that.' Titus held out his hand for the teacup she was still holding and sniffed that too.

'Oh shit. I think it's aconite. Look!' There was an overturned teapot on the draining-board and some scattered leaves among the grit. He licked his finger, pressed it on a leaf, tasted it and spat.

'It's aconite or Christmas Rose. Deadly, if you don't know what you're doing.' He looked back in horror at Bitty's dreadful face.

'But it couldn't kill someone?'

'It can cause suffocation, respiratory failure, epileptic seizures, hallucination . . .'

She cut through his litany of dreadful deaths with a scream. 'Why the hell do you grow it?'

'Dunno,' Titus said miserably. 'It's pretty.'

Minou sent him to find something clean for Bitty to put on.

'Be careful on the stairs, there may be aftershock.' He came back with a pink bathrobe.

'We can't leave her here. Help.'

An ankle each, they pulled her out from behind the kitchen table then looked at one another.

'Now what?'

'We could put her in the deep freeze,' Titus suggested. Minou said that was ridiculous and anyway impractical since the electricity was off. She fought a hysterical impulse to giggle.

'What about the salon?' Whatever happened, she wasn't going to leave Bitty on those filthy tiles. 'Help me.' They struggled with her over a pile of bricks towards the salon door. With all the life gone out of her she was even heavier.

'I thought one wasn't supposed to move the body?' Titus gasped.

'That's only for murder, stupid. Look out!' He was backing into the twelve apostles sideboard. 'Over there.' They laid her down where the table used to be. She made him turn his back as she pulled the soiled housecoat off Bitty's still supple body.

'Get rid of this.' She handed him the disgusting garment.

'The evidence?' Out of sheer nerves he couldn't resist his Colombo voice. After all, it was only a nightmare, the Datura hadn't quite worn off and was giving him one final kickback test. Later on he'd soar to glory. He went outside and chucked the housecoat in the bin on top of the dead rat, found some broken china and squashed oranges, piled them high and jammed the bin lid on.

'I'm going to check out the dogs,' he called in a thin voice and went off trying to whistle for them.

Alone with Bitty in the salon, Minou's sense of humour froze. Something that had been tapping in her mind began to knock louder. It wasn't quite there but dangerously close. She looked down at her half-sister. If she'd been pissed, which she obviously was, she wouldn't have known the difference between Christmas Rose and cocoa. It could be divine retribution of some sort. Then cold suspicion broke its cover. Titus could have done it! He and she had nothing but a history of hate and hurt. He had a motive. The house was nearly gone. Furthermore, he had a lot of Latin blood. With all these appalling thoughts she ran into the kitchen, grabbed a pail and with shaking hands filled it from the gushing pipe in the debris of the pantry. Ankle deep in brown water she searched for the Parazone. If he'd done it and it *was* the levante it would only count as manslaughter. That's what they said. But did it count three days after? Four days before? Teeth clenched against her own bile, she threw bucket after bucket on the floor, trying to remember when the wind had stopped. Would they take into account a total eclipse of a full summer moon? Like a maniac Minou worked, water and dust turning to mud, she squirted Parazone in all directions and threw pail after pail of filthy water through the space in the wall. Defeated, she chucked the mop into the corner and filled the pail for the last time, very carefully rinsed the cup and teapot and set them on the draining-board where they sat looking suspiciously un-dusty. There was just one more thing . . . Quaking with apprehension and disgust she took the pail into the salon.

The dogs were all accounted for. The labradors, hackles up, crouched by the Range Rover, whining at each other in a sad duet. The greyhound shivered violently, every vein upstanding under its thin skin. Titus found the Peke eventually. It was fast asleep under the beach buggy and it hadn't heard a thing.

'Stay, stay.' They collected in a puzzled, hopeful row. Titus went back into the salon. Bitty, watched over by twelve apostles, was all cleaned up and in her bathrobe. Her hands were folded on her breast and her frightening, last gasp face was covered with the *Sunday Times*. Gently they closed the door on her and went to sit beneath the fig tree in the drive. Minou asked Titus if he had a cigarette.

'Oughtn't we to call someone?'

'Like who?' Her hands were shaking and her voice was hardly there.

'A doctor? The Guardia?' In the distance they could hear the sound of sirens.

'They'll come soon enough.' The thought filled her with a new terror.

'It was all my fault.' He spoke in a dull voice that came from just beneath his skin.

'What do you mean?'

'The gods must have heard.' As he told her of his prayers and supplications and how the gods had listened to him, she shook her head in shame for her suspicions and held him as he wept and told her that he never thought they'd take him seriously.

Ingrid arrived first, hurling herself out of her Beetle with a portable radio blaring excited Spanish and static. She was followed almost immediately by two motorcycle Guardia with dark glasses. They switched off their sirens and drew up either side of her car.

'The Rock's gone!' she cried and ran towards Titus and threw her arms around him.

'We know.' Titus rose, sounding as offhand as he could and detached himself from Ingrid. Ingrid gave the mountain where El Bueno's hole spilled earth like blood a cursory glance.

'Not that rock, The Rock!' She gestured towards Gibraltar and shook the radio which had six languages intermixing.

'Serves it right.' Titus cheered up immediately and walked with dignity and an outstretched hand towards the Guardia, who took off their dark glasses. He wished he had his own at hand to hide the purple tear stains around his eyes and heaven only knew what that scar was doing.

'Is everyone all right?' one of the policemen asked

him while the other looked around as though for fingerprints.

'Yes,' he assured them. 'Well, not quite everyone.' The radio went into total static. Ingrid shook it and got a Mozart requiem from Brussels. 'We need a doctor, quickly.'

'Is someone hurt?'

'Not exactly. Dead.'

'Then there is no hurry. The roads are closed, it might take time.' But he started to talk fast into his walkie-talkie. The other one started to check out the house and make notes. For the first time Titus noticed the damage. As the two policemen circled the house and viewed the body Titus and Minou sat down again under the fig tree. Despite their protestations, Ingrid turned the Beetle and headed down the drive to the bar to get some brandy.

'That leaves just you and me, and the house,' he said to her. 'What's left of it.' It was just beginning to feel like quite a good idea.

'No, Titus,' she said gently. 'Just you.' And she told him what she'd done.

They felt it in Tarifa. At the Central, plates and glasses tinkled, cutlery danced off the tables and pigeons swooped in startled flocks around Guzman the Good. A stone cherub tumbled off the church. Tom was in the postcard shop, which doubled for ProntoPrint, vegetables and suntan oil. Across the road he could see Jimmy and Bonker in deep conversation about bilge pumps.

'Hair of the dog!' Jimmy had insisted when relinquished by the nuns at the clinic with tender smiles and giggles and sporting a bright, white cast on his arm. Two Spaniards cycling past shouted out to Bonker the equivalent of 'What Ho!' Bonker's mouth followed the droop of his zapata moustache. Without Bonquette, life had no meaning and the town was too small for him. Tom left them to it. He wasn't in the mood for post-mortems. ProntoPrint said Ingrid's film would be ready soon. But he was in no hurry as he found his thoughts eagerly embracing a life at sea with Minou, which puzzled him. For the first time in his life a commitment hadn't filled him with blind panic. He tried to read a Spanish newspaper. The girl had to ask him twice if he'd mind moving from the fax machine.

'Sorry.' The photographs were ready in ten minutes. Ingrid certainly knew her job. She'd captured Minou's half smile, slim hands, her smothered giggle as she exchanged a look with Juanita, and the wary way she distanced herself from Desmond. But, he had to admit, she was no photographer herself. The snap she'd taken of Ingrid and Titus was a disaster, badly framed, out of focus, her shadow centred on them. But the background was sharp, the statue as bright as if it had been studio lit. That statue again. Tom studied the picture for a full minute. Then bought a pad and a Biro.

He wrote a note to one of the Carolines. The one who'd worked on the 'Antiques Road Show'. The girl made a copy of the snap. He asked her for some scissors and cut out Titus and Ingrid. The enlargement of the statue was surprisingly clear. The girl said she had to send a couple of faxes for the patron first.

'How long?' She shrugged and said it was difficult to tell as the machine seldom worked on Thursdays. At least, that's what he thought she said. She smiled and took his name and address and said she'd do it for him as soon as she could. At that moment the shop shuddered. Potatoes rolled on to the floor and the fax machine stopped. They looked at each other with blank faces. Outside on the street people stared with disbelief at the sky. Some of the Feria lights snapped off and crashed on to a rooftop. An old lady in black threw herself face down on the road and nearly got run over. He heard someone shouting '*El bojeo!*' He started to run for the car.

CHAPTER ELEVEN

THE BELL TOLLED for Bitty in Tarifa. Soft blue and red reflections from the stained glass window of St Michael dappled the white wreath on her coffin. It was from Desmond, a testament of wealth. Roses, orchids, stephanotis and lilies of the valley (flown in at dawn from Holland to Constance Spry in Marbella) and dispatched via Holt, who'd been told to make himself useful. Desmond also sent a note to Titus saying how very sad he was not to be with him in his hour of grief, but that he'd been unavoidably detained on business in Madrid, and hoped they'd meet again soon. The congregation in the large church was sparse, the few official mourners in a little group near the altar. But, as was the custom in the town, most of the elderly dropped in to shuffle round, if not paying respects, at least to find out who it was that was on their way. The splendour of the four-foot wreath brought murmurs of awe and admiration as the scent of the lilies mingled with the incense. Minou thought how sad it was that Bitty didn't know about the wreath. Her supreme moment too late. Maybe it was best that way. At least she'd been spared the humiliation of disintegrating fantasies. If there was a heaven, and Minou suspended her agnostic tendencies for a moment, Bitty would know all about it anyway.

'*In Spirito Sancti . . .*' She knelt down as the priest went about his business. He was still a little puzzled by the irregularity of it all – no last rites – but then it was hardly the fault of the deceased. Yet the request for a service had come as a surprise since Señora Nolan hadn't set foot in the church in the twenty years she'd lived there.

'Put her down as Catholic,' Titus had said firmly, dealing with the question which arose when filling in the death certificate with Dr Cordoba. Dr Cordoba was going on for eighty and had only recently heard of penicillin. Remembering 'All Things Bright And Beautiful' and the vicar who'd taken Sunday school in Hastings, and absolutely sure that Bitty had never converted, Minou started to say so.

'But—'

'Got to get 'em under by sunset the following day. Spanish law.' Titus shut her up with rapid English. 'Unless there's an inquest.' To do otherwise would have meant informing the British Consul in Malaga (who'd got wind of it anyway and sent a spray of gladioli), endless red tape, finding mortuaries for an eventual C of E burial in Gibraltar. Not even Bitty deserved to be dispatched in Gibraltar. Across the aisle, Dr Cordoba yawned, his old eyes watering with fatigue rather than sorrow. The Feria was always busy and he was getting past it. Three stabbings this year, two concussions, six complaints of food poisoning, for the most part overindulgence, and Mrs Nolan's heart attack. To say nothing of the earth tremor which brought a rush of minor cuts and bruises. As the Kyrie eleison rose softly to the rafters Dr Cordoba nodded off. Minou closed her eyes, still drowsy from the sedative he'd given her the night before. She'd slept for twelve hours. When she woke she thought the earthquake had started again. Everything was white and shining, sun glinting on outsize scent bottles left behind by Mrs Delahaye. She was on the *Dancing Lady* and Tom was asleep beside her, his arm across her breasts. Using the quietness as a cover she lay still, happy with the moment and not needing to know why. Until Tom moved and pulled her closer.

'Would it be silly to ask: how did this happen?'

'The earth moved, don't you remember?' The boat rocked from side to side, waves slapping up against the hull. Refusing separation he slid inside her, moving gently until they took possession of each other. As the Kyrie eleison faded to its last, Minou pulled herself reluctantly out of her shamefully erotic reverie. Tom was sitting with the pallbearers with a faraway look on his face. She'd never asked him about his spiritual beliefs, that was if he had any. But if he had, she was convinced that he was a man who lived what he believed at the moment of the doing. Like Jean Luc. Still kneeling she gave thanks to Whoever for sending her a man who'd never tear the wings off butterflies and then a prayer for those, like Bitty, whirling round so lonely in the world.

The pallbearers rose to carry Bitty for her final ride: Titus, Tom, Bonker and the Notario. Antonio had been mortally offended when his offer was tactfully deflected due to the discrepancy in height. These men needed to be strong. Tom had volunteered in place of Jimmy, whose broken arm had ruled him out, despite his genuinely good intentions. As the coffin settled on their shoulders there was the creaking sound of tearing stitches. Tom, whose sense of rightness wouldn't allow him to wear jeans, had done serious battle with his vanity when lent a suit by Annie Mason's Arnold, a small man with a big waist. He took care not to look at his legs which revealed eight inches of blue sock before the trousers started. As Minou rose, pulling down the grey mini-dress lent by Ingrid to a more decorous length, Tom caught her movement and glanced at her, sharing a second of shameless lust – noted by Annie Mason. Bonker, looking neither right nor left, carried his burden past Bonquette as though it was indeed she who was in the coffin. Bonquette, surrounded by female in-laws and heavily draped in black lace, sobbed for her lost love. Aware of Annie Mason's eyes on her legs, Minou fell behind and gave Saint Michael one last look. If there was a heaven, Bitty and Jean Luc would have met by now. He'd sort her out.

The undertakers relieved the pallbearers of the coffin which they slid expertly into the waiting hearse. Under Titus's instruction it moved off to wait discreetly in a side street. Across the road the Central was filling up for an impromptu wake. Annie Mason had cried off because of Arnold's legs. The Mayor popped out of his office to give his condolences. Two of the nuns from the medical clinic got quite merry with Jimmy, who kept forgetting it was a funeral. There were several ladies from the 'Dog In Danger Society' who shared reminiscences of Bitty's kindness to animals with anyone who would listen, stories which ran their course quite quickly, overtaken by buzz about the tremor. Nothing like it since they'd felt the earthquake in Agadir in the sixties. Someone's barn had collapsed, someone's goats had run amok. To Titus's deep disgust and disappointment Gibraltar had not fallen. They showed it on television, the north side draped in bright green nylon hair nets to catch the few rocks which had slithered down. His grave sadness as he received the murmur of condolence hid very suitably his disappointment that Nature had got it wrong. Dr Cordoba shook hands with Juanita, who he was convinced was Bitty's mother. His wife led him away.

'We haven't told Helen!' Titus and Minou looked at each other with guilt and panic, appalled at how quickly Bitty had been cancelled out. Someone reminded them that the telephones were out of action. The manager of the Reina Christina stepped in and offered Titus the use of a room (almost free), for as long as it would be of use to him. The antique dealer from Jerez sidled up to have a quick word about the twelve apostles sideboard.

'Done.' Titus, who had no idea how he was going to pay the funeral expenses, shook hands on the deal. He signalled to Holt across the road, standing underneath the repair work of the Feria lights.

'Do you want me to come with you?' Minou offered.

'No. Wait for me here.' Holt opened the door of the Rolls for him. They set off at a dignified pace after the hearse. As they passed, people doffed their caps and crossed themselves.

The headland cemetery was reserved for foreigners, most of them Moroccan sailors or refugees drowned in cockleshell boats as they attempted the treacherous currents of the Straits crossing. The grave was dug, the coffin lowered into the red earth. The priest tinkled his bell for the last time and looked expectantly at Titus. He took a clod of earth and let it patter on to the coffin. It was a pity Bitty had put that Jack Russell down so quickly or she could have had it with her for company. A slim dark figure against the sullen red sky, Titus swept her a bow worthy of the Great Manolo and silently told Bitty that he was sorry, but he'd done his best.

'Where to, sir?' asked Holt.

'The Café Central.'

'I could take you home, sir.'

Titus told him he'd rather take the bus.

Annie Mason had beaten them to it. They arrived back at the house to find her shoving the greyhound along with the other dogs into the back of the Rover. Juanita, smelling trouble, had followed her. Hands on hips, eyes alight with fire not kindled since she was a girl, she had a lot to say very quickly, repeating the word *gallinazo* with scorching vehemence. *Gallinazo, gallinazo* . . . vulture! For a moment they thought the birds had returned until Titus noticed the bundles of Bitty's clothes on the front seat.

'I promised Bitty if anything ever happened I'd take care of the dogs.' Annie managed to sob as she gave the fattest labrador a final shove and shut the door. 'It was an agreement we had. "Bitty," I said, "you can trust me."' Titus refrained from saying they must both have been totally sloshed.

'She'd have done the same for me.' Titus looked at the clothes again. Juanita, unable to contain her fury any longer, told him she'd only just been able to prevent the woman from plundering the linen cupboard and pinching stacks of toilet paper from the downstairs lavatory. Annie turned a strange ochre colour.

'Well, you won't be needing them, will you? I'll give them to the Save Our Four-Footed Friends jumble sale. She'd have done the same for me.' She banged the dogs' plates into the boot and closed it.

'I'm sure she would,' Titus assured her in a kindly

but absent way, adding, 'she didn't have much in the way of jewellery, though.' He'd already checked. A diamond engagement ring she'd not worn since her fingers got too plump, and an amethyst brooch with a broken clasp and a thin string of seed pearls that was probably a christening present. Annie, crimson, tossed her head and got into the car and revved more than necessary. As he was sure Bitty would have done.

They walked round the garden. The official surveyor for the Junta de Cadiz had, over-cautiously, declared the house unsafe. The men were already boarding up and banging on the kitchen wall. There wasn't much damage except the flattened trail El Bueno had left. It had just missed the statue, now fallen on its side. Minou bent down to heave it back to standing.

'Oh, leave it.' He came back from deep thought. 'I never liked it anyway.'

'Why not? It's rather nice. It reminds me of you.'

'Have it then. Something to remember me by.' There was a wild appeal in his voice. A statue was the last thing that she needed. 'But they'll never let me take it on the boat.' Men were men and became curiously irate on the subject of women and luggage.

'Crate it up. Say it's booze, they'll never know the difference.' He jerked his head to the thudding coming from outside the kitchen. 'They'll do it for you.'

'OK.' Minou forgot about it instantly, her mind ahead with Tom and sailing home.

'I'd better get my things.' They started back towards the house.

'Are you going?' He looked as if it was unthinkable.

'You know I am, Titus. Quite soon. Something to do with winds.' He watched her brave the creaking stairs and went to tell the men to crate the statue. Minou shoved her things in her case and went to the balcony for one last time. The men were carrying the statue to their tool kits.

'Why don't you come and have dinner with me and Tom?' Minou called down as she folded up the cashmere sweater. Tom and me, so secure, coupled and complete. Titus shook his head.

'I promised Ingrid,' he said, vaguely remembering that at his request she'd valiantly agreed to have a stab at shepherd's pie and apple crumble.

For the next hour he wandered around the silent salon, the upstairs rooms and then back into the garden. It was his home but there was no delight. A flock of storks flew past the red cavity left by El Bueno. He went down to the bamboo grove and stared silently at the two great pieces of rock, two halves of a solid, grey egg. The wind changed. A light cool breeze rustled through the yellow stalks. He remembered that he had to phone Helen. He walked quickly back to the house, packed up his own clothes and collected Cody's videos, stacked for years behind 'Wildlife On One' at the back of the apostle sideboard.

CHAPTER TWELVE

AFTER SEVERAL TRIAL runs with Bonker at the helm, the *Dancing Lady* was declared as sweet as sugar. It was decided that Bonker should come too. He'd made it very clear that within days, hours maybe, unless he made a drastic change in his life he would either shoot himself, Bonquette, or Bonquette's husband or perhaps all three. It solved the problem with Jimmy's arm and Tom was deeply relieved to have Bonker aboard. At least he knew how to get to the Canary Islands. Jimmy's arm had in no way diminished his enthusiasm but Tom had had a difficult time persuading him not to complete his image with an eye-patch and parrot. While the two able-bodied crew made themselves useful with heavy loads and ropes, Jimmy sat on deck on a crate of baked beans ticking off the stores as Tom humped them aboard: dried milk powdered eggs, olive oil, sardines, dried apricots, rice, vitamin C, Alka-Seltzer, Dettol, Fairy liquid, lavatory paper, at Bonker's request a carton of Cadbury's Fruit and Nut, for which he'd developed a craving, corned beef . . .

'Why corned beef?' Tom argued. 'We never eat it on dry land.'

'One eats corned beef at sea.' Jimmy was insufferably knowledgeable. 'Where are the potatoes?' Tom went back on shore to get them.

Minou sat in the saloon, a writing pad on her knee, while Ingrid arranged some roses in a jug.

Dear Madame . . .

Ingrid asked if there were any bowls for several kilos of oranges, peaches and tangerines. 'Or you can get scurvy,' she sounded glum.

'In the kitchen – galley.' Minou corrected herself quickly.

'*What the hell is that?*' Minou looked up at Jimmy's shout. There was a sound of grunting. Something thudded on to the deck. A large crate with Rioja stencilled on the side and painted underneath, 'Not Needed On Voyage'. Titus looked at him, slightly hurt.

'It's wine, it's a present.' Jimmy said there was a problem about balancing the weight. Bonker offered to put it in his cabin and Jimmy, who couldn't bring himself to reject a gift of booze, gave in. There was more grunting as Bonker and Titus manœuvred the crate down the narrow companionway. Minou thought it best to ignore the whole thing.

Dear Madame,

In a few moments we set sail for Martinique but we have to go to the Canaries first.

She hadn't been able to see why they should take such a long way around but Tom showed her a batch of arrows swirling around a map and told her they were trade winds and absolutely essential.

There are four of us, two brothers and an ex-merchant seaman. Just as well because he knows about boats and not sure that the others do. But dear Madame, remember what you said about passion and literature? And about love? Couldn't they be the same thing? Just this once? I'll write again as soon as I can.

Love, Minou

'Well, that's that.' She asked Ingrid to post it for her. Ingrid's lip trembled. Jimmy caught sight of her.

'Don't put flowers in a vase, woman. And what the hell are those oranges doing lying around loose? Don't you realise that she moves about?' While Ingrid was shoving fruit into plastic bags and desperately trying to find hooks to hang them on, Titus popped his head around the saloon door.

'Done it,' he said. 'It's in Bonker's cabin.' A bell rang.

'What's that mean?'

'I think it means we're leaving.'

'All aboard!' shouted Jimmy. Everyone was but for Bonker, who was on the quayside loosening the painter from the bollards.

'We'd better go, then.' There was a nervous flurry of anticipation; the men, looking serious, set about their tasks. Minou, Titus and Ingrid stood on deck. Minou held on to to Titus, who held her back as if he'd never breathe again without her.

'Come on.' Ingrid took him by the arm and guided him down the gangplank as if he was an invalid. Bonker released the last warp and leaped aboard as nimbly as a cat. The space between the bow and the quay widened smoothly.

'Take care! I'll write. Come and see us. Come back

soon.' Minou leaned on the rail. At first their voices were conversational, stilted, shy, then louder until suddenly they were out of earshot and could only wave.

'We can wave again from the hotel,' suggested Ingrid, who was still holding the roses. Titus stared at the boat making the harbour mouth, then turning left out into the Straits. A motor scooter in great haste roared past them and stopped just short of the water's edge. Antonio leaped off and stared in despair at the disappearing boat.

'Señor Tom! Señor Tom!' he shouted, jumping up and down and waving a bit of paper. 'Señor Tom!' His voice rose into a beseeching wail. 'Oh, too late, too late . . .' He fell to his knees, pounding the ground. Titus helped him to his feet. Antonio, still gesturing with the piece of paper, jumped up and down trying to see over his shoulder. Beside himself with shame, he slumped, a torrent of woe streaming from him, about the lady at ProntoPrint, how she'd trusted him, it was important paper for Señor Tom. Titus took it from him and read it. A moment later he burst into a cracked gasp then a laugh overtook him. He read the paper again, held his arms over his stomach as he heaved with helpless, wicked joy. Tears ran down his face.

'Yahoo!' He threw his black hat into the water.

'What's so funny?' Ingrid couldn't see anything to laugh at.

'Listen, listen.' He read her the fax, Caroline's return fax to Tom. 'If it's going cheap, grab it. Professional opinion pretty unanimous. Bronze of boy with dog, most likely Greco, not, repeat not, Greco Roman. Possibly one of a pair, the other discovered near Trafalgar in 1928, now in British Museum. If it's a genuine Praxilites you're talking about 6.5 million (pounds). You lucky sod. Love, Caroline.'

'I could have told you that,' said Ingrid.

They argued on the balcony of the Reina Christina about what to do, waving absently from time to time at the progressing boat.

'Why aren't you going to tell Minou? We could radio them.'

Titus shook his head. 'No.'

'But why not?'

'It would spoil it for her,' he said wisely. It would be too cruel to suddenly tell her that she'd sailed off with the treasure of La Preciosa in Bonker's cabin.'

'What do you mean, spoil it for her? I don't think it's morally correct not to tell her.'

'It's got nothing to do with morals. The damn thing's been there for ages.' It could have been there since the pirate built the house, although in Titus's opinion it was most likely found by Cody's props man. 'Morals don't come into it unless you're a die-hard materialist.' This cut Ingrid, a deeply devout socialist since she was weaned, to the quick.

'Excuse me, sir, you're wanted on the telephone.' The waiter interrupted what was about to be their first row. 'Sir Desmond Macmahon.'

'Holy shit!' Desmond had been calling twice a day since he moved into the hotel. He hadn't felt like talking to him. Didn't know what to say. But now he did.

The two American women who'd eyed him without shame the week before were checking out. Smooth and bronzed in expensively crushed and crumpled linen, surrounded by Louis Vuitton luggage, one of them was arguing about the bill. The telephonist told Titus she was trying to reconnect his call. He lit a cigarette.

'What do you mean you can't take Gold Card?' The American hovered between outrage, sweet reason and charm. The other one left her to it and closed in on Titus.

'We meet again,' she murmured.

'Do we?' He drew a blank.

'How cute. Don't you remember?' The telephonist was shouting at Madrid.

'Yes, of course,' he said.

'You really ought to come to LA,' she said, blatantly pulling out her wallet and her card. 'If you do, look me up. It would be fun.' She gave him the card. 'Don't you have a name?' she chided. He forced himself to think about it for a moment, a name, yes of course he had a name.

'Titus.' Which grandfather to tack on? She smiled at him.

'Titus, Manolo . . . Cody,' he added as an after-thought.

'Cody as in Cody?' Her well-plucked eyebrows arched with interest.

'Your call, sir.' The telephonist motioned him into the brocade-covered phone booth.

'Excuse me.'

'So cute,' sighed the American as he closed himself into the cubicle.

The telephonist told him not to go away. He looked at himself in the mirror above the ivory phone, left profile, right profile, wondered, if well lit, his scar would show and if it was old-fashioned for stars to insist on showing their good side. But it was hardly there, only visible if he pulled the skin on his cheek. Then again, a scar, if treated with reverence, could become a trade mark.

'Hullo, Titus.' It was Desmond at his oiliest. He said that he realised it was probably not the best of moments, that he hated to intrude on him at this time but had he given any thought as to whether the deal over La Preciosa still held? Titus turned vague and said there was a bit of damage to the kitchen. Desmond, who'd already had a report to this effect, waved it away. The garden he asked, how was the garden? A stupid question as the garden had been a tip for twenty years. Titus screwed the fax into a tight ball in his pocket. Come on, you bastard! Come on!

'The garden? Oh, much the same.' He managed to sound bored. Desmond then asked him if he'd accept a proposal? A bit unorthodox, but seeing they were friends. He said he knew the law took its own time but he for one was prepared to forgo all those formalities which were in fact nothing but hindrances. What need for probate?

'What indeed?' Titus agreed, holding his breath.

'Well,' suggested Desmond and said he'd send a money order for the full amount agreed with Bitty to Titus's bank, that afternoon. Now. Cash. Which bank?

'Which bank?' He'd had an overdraft of twenty pounds for the last two years which from time to time invoked letters that under any other circumstances would have been considered worthy of prosecution for extortion with menaces. It seemed a shame to let that pig of a bank manager get his hands on anything but it wouldn't be for long. In fact he'd let him sniff it, then take it out immediately.

'Which bank, Titus?'

'The Banco D'España, Plaza dos Torres, Algeciras.' They agreed to have a nice, quiet dinner somewhere very soon. Titus put down the receiver.

'Gotcha!' he shouted.

* * *

Ingrid drove at a stolid 25 mph staring at the white line in the middle of the road as if by concentrating on it the events of the last few hours would unfold into something she could understand.

'But, I thought you loved the house?' she ventured. If she mentioned the ethics of the statue, Titus would accuse her of being a capitalist again, not that she could see that politics had anything to do with it. 'Don't you?'

'Don't I what?' Titus gave her an absent attention.

'Love the house?'

He fiddled with her binoculars, trying to catch a glimpse of the boat in the patches of sea between the cork trees.

'Don't you?'

'Of course I do.' He was staring out to sea.

'Then why did you sell it?'

'Because.' Because with Bitty gone it was so quiet. The Lobelia hung in dried, grey drifts, the hum of the deep freeze had been silenced and the only sound was the patter of plaster which fell with every step he took. Ingrid drove on without speaking until they reached the headland. They got out and leaned against the overheated Beetle. The seven hill ridges to Marrakesh were sharp and clear, the wind was sweet and warm. Titus, it seemed to Ingrid, was haloed by a great wildness.

'I'm going to Hollywood,' he told her, still looking through the binoculars.

'Ah.' She always knew something like this would happen, but not quite so soon. She looked at her watch, measuring time left.

'Well,' he said, 'Everyone's going somewhere, or gone somewhere.'

'I haven't,' she pointed out.

'That's different. You're brainy.' For the life of her she couldn't follow his reasoning but there was no point in trying. Titus was already gone, shining in the spotlight of his future.

'Look! There they are! Wave!' The boat came into view, three sails, long pointed triangles of white, above the sleek hull. Ingrid took her binoculars from him. Through her tears the sails became three white blurs.

'Do you think they can see us?' Titus jumped up and down waving his arms. 'Wave! Wave!' As she passed the cemetery her Union Jack slid to half mast for a moment then fluttered up again as the *Dancing Lady* dipped gracefully into the Atlantic.